BOWIE'S MINE

**Center Point
Large Print**

**This Large Print Book carries the
Seal of Approval of N.A.V.H.**

BOWIE'S MINE

Elmer Kelton

CENTER POINT PUBLISHING
THORNDIKE, MAINE

This Center Point Large Print edition
is published in the year 2007 by arrangement with
St. Martin's Press.

The text of this Large Print edition is unabridged. In other
aspects, this book may vary from the original edition. Printed in
Thailand. Set in 16-point Times New Roman type.

ISBN-10: 1-60285-004-6
ISBN-13: 978-1-60285-004-0

Library of Congress Cataloging-in-Publication Data

Kelton, Elmer.
    Bowie's mine / Elmer Kelton.--Center Point large print ed.
      p. cm.
    ISBN-13: 978-1-60285-004-0 (lib. bdg. : alk. paper)
    1. Silver mines and mining--Fiction. 2. Texas--History--Republic, 1836-1846--Fiction.
    3. Large type books. I. Title.

PS3561.E3975B69 2007
813'.54--dc22

2007002139

1

HIS NAME WAS DANIEL PROVOST, AND IT WAS THE time of the Texas Republic. Once, years ago, he had heard Sam Houston's Twin Sister cannons at San Jacinto, and from sanctuary beyond the rain-flooded bayous he had watched smoke rise over the battlefield. He had been a boy then, too young to fight. Now the 1840's were well along and he was a man, but no adventure was left. Modern times and civilization seemed to have stilled it forever. His world was restricted to the narrow confines of Hopeful Valley along the Colorado River in what was considered western Texas, and it was seen mostly over the narrow-pinched rump of a lazy brown mule.

The man riding the bay horse and leading three packmules was the first stranger Daniel had seen in three months. Daniel leaned to pull against the leather reins looped around the back of his neck and let the heavy wooden plow ease over as he watched the horseman slowly work his way down the gentle hill toward the field. The man wore buckskin and an old Mexican sombrero that had seen too many rains, and too much sun. Daniel watched in silent curiosity as the man reined up at the end of the plowed rows and raised his hand in peace.

The man's longrifle lay across his lap, but Daniel saw no threat in it. The face looked friendly enough,

5

what he could see of it through a considerable growth of brown whiskers.

"Stand there, Hezekiah," Daniel needlessly admonished the mule; any time Hez was given a chance to halt, he wouldn't lift a foot until he had to. Daniel slipped out of the reins and trudged across the rows, studying the man. "How do. Anything I can do for you?"

The man looked around, and Daniel sensed he was searching for sign of a rifle. Daniel had none. The man said, "I come in peace, brother, as any good and honorable man." A benign smile shone through the whiskers, and Daniel could see this was a young man, thirty possibly, maybe even less. "Name's Milo Seldom. Is that water you got in yonder jug, or somethin' stronger?"

"Water," said Daniel, and fetched the canvas-wrapped jug from where it hung in the benevolent shade of a huge and ancient live oak.

"Sure am obliged," said Seldom, and tipped the jug off his shoulder in the style of a man drinking whisky. He took several long draws, then wiped his sleeve across his mouth and handed back the jug. "Mighty good water. Many a place I been, folks'll offer you hard liquor first off; glad to see that you-all here have got a bent toward religion."

Daniel shrugged. "Ain't religion, exactly. Whisky and hot sun and hard work don't mix too good. My name's Daniel Provost. You come a long ways?"

"A long ways. Still got a fair piece to go." He

pointed his chin. "Seen a cabin as I topped the hill. You got a wife there, and family?"

"Ain't married. I live with my folks."

"Seen a deer back yonder a mile or so. If I was to go fetch it in, reckon the woman of the house might see fit to share vittles with a lonesome, hungry stranger?"

"You don't need to bring nothin' to be welcome at the Provost house." But Daniel reckoned it wouldn't hurt any; the menfolks had been too busy with the planting to fetch fresh meat.

"I always like to bring more than I take away," the stranger said. "Leaves folks thinkin' good of ol' Milo Seldom. If you'd kindly see after my packmules a bit, I'd go see after that there deer."

Daniel took the lead rope and led the mules to the tree where he had kept the water jug. Knowing mules, he didn't put the jug back where it had been. Hezekiah moved his head interestedly, looking at the packmules and watching Seldom ride away on his bay horse. But he showed no inclination to move his feet; he never did until he was forced to.

Daniel studied the bulging packs and tried to make out the vague aroma that came from them. It was somehow familiar, but mixed with the strong mule-sweat it was too evasive to identify. Curiosity nagged at him, and when the stranger was out of sight, Daniel went so far as to put a hand on the rope that held one canvas bundle. But he changed his mind; a man didn't poke where he had no business. He walked back to Hez and put him and the plow into service again, his mind on the stranger rather than on the job. He sensed that Seldom had come from far-off places, and maybe was headed for far-off places Daniel hadn't even heard of, let alone seen.

Daniel had no fear of work, and the plow-handle fit his hands, but he had often thought it would be good, just once before he settled finally into harness and took up wife and land of his own, to go out and see what lay beyond the hills that rimmed this valley; to see the lands from which the few travelers came; perhaps even to see the mysterious western country from which the Comanches used to materialize wraithlike to strike suddenly and kill and burn and fade away again.

He sensed that Milo Seldom had been to these places—some of them, anyway—and that his hands were not made for the plow. Briefly he envied the man as he had envied a couple of men in Hopeful Valley who had been in the thick of the battle with Sam Houston. They never talked about it much; they talked much easier about crops and horses and cattle and the like. Maybe that was the way of it for most men—one big adventure and they were ready to settle down for a quiet, steady life of hard work. Trouble was, Daniel hadn't had his adventure yet. He sensed that Milo Seldom was a man given entirely to the kind of experience Daniel hungered after.

Before long he heard the crack of the longrifle. There was no second shot, which did not surprise Daniel; he suspected those keen gray eyes needed but one chance to look down the barrel and over the sights. By the time the stranger came back, the deer properly gutted and draped behind his saddle, Daniel had finished to the end of a row. The sun was still an hour high, but on such an occasion as having a stranger call, he doubted that anybody could fault him for calling it a day. He unhitched Hezekiah from the plow, climbed up onto his bare back and rode to the tree where the packmules were tied.

The stranger sat idly pitching up a flattened chunk of lead and catching it in his hand. It was the ball which he had used to kill the deer. Lead was not to be wasted, and a hunter usually made every effort to retrieve it and melt it to be poured for another day, another deer.

Daniel said, "You just shot once."

"Poverty makes a man a good shot. Takes coin for powder and lead, and precious little coin ever crosses my palm. But it's a-fixin' to, my friend."

"What do you mean?" Daniel knew it wasn't any of his business, but the stranger had opened the subject.

"Them packs there, they're goin' to open the door. I'm goin' to find out if gettin' rich spoils a man's shootin' eye."

"You need any help?" Daniel joked.

The stranger took him seriously. "Matter of fact, I just might, was the right man to come along."

Daniel stopped smiling. "You didn't say whichaway you was headed."

Seldom eyed him a moment in silence. "Was headed

for your house to find out if your kind mother would like some fresh venison."

Daniel took that as a sign that the subject was closed, and he didn't press it. But as he rode he glanced back at those big packs, jouncing along on the quick-footed Mexican mules. He noted the easy, almost slouchy way Seldom rode, as if he had been hatched in a horse barn. But if his riding was slouchy, his gray eyes were searching.

"Ain't nothin' here you got to watch out for," Daniel told him. "Last Indian trouble we had was several years ago. Just a little bunch huntin' for horses, mostly."

"Them Indians ain't dissolved off of the face of the earth, friend Provost. Just because there's more settlement now than there used to be don't mean they won't show up again; more settlement means more horses. Indian, he always has a powerful want for more horses."

"I'll bet you've fought Indians."

"Ain't we all? Fought Mexicans, fought outlaws, fought bears and cougars. Fought sin, too. Life's an eternal struggle for the right thinkin' and the true believer."

"You sound like a preacher."

"I ain't, but now and again when I find somebody in need of the Word, I carry it to them the way it's been carried to me. Figure I owe it to folks to pass on the blessin's I've received. You strike me as bein' a good true Christian, Mister Provost."

"Name's Daniel," Daniel reminded him. "I've read the Book. Never done no hard studyin' on it, though."

"Man don't have to study it; it's all around him—in the blue sky, in the green hills full of game, in the runnin' streams and the rivers full of fish. The Lord's work is all around us plainer than words in a book. Ain't everybody can read a book, but anybody can see the Lord's good work."

That led Daniel to wonder if Seldom could even read; lots of people couldn't. There wasn't a great call for reading in this country anyway; long as a man could do a few ciphers and plow a straight furrow and sight down a barrel, they would have to get up awful early to starve him to death. It was often said that Texas was overrun with lawyers and bookish people; what it needed was men who knew how to build something and bring in food and fiber. The educated folk were considered like scavengers who took secondhand what someone else's labor had wrought.

Daniel observed, "The Indian is part of God's work too, I guess."

Seldom grunted. "Put here to test us. The good Lord gave us the gun to shoot him with."

Daniel nodded. "I reckon."

Seldom studied Daniel's brown mule and the tangle of harness. "You don't carry a gun to the field with you?"

"Last three-four years ain't been no need. The only feathers we ever see any more are on wild turkeys."

Seldom gave him a look that plainly said he doubted

a farmer was apt to be much of a shot anyway. Daniel took this as a challenge. He said, "You mind if I try a shot with that old longrifle of yours?"

Seldom stared at him in doubt. "Ol' Betsy's a shade contrary." It was fashion for Texans to name their rifles after the one David Crockett had carried into the Alamo. "Keep in mind that she bears a hair to the left." He poured powder into the pan and handed the rifle to Daniel as Daniel slid off the mule. Daniel picked a dead limb on a lightning-struck live oak fifty yards away and dropped to one knee. The pan flashed, the rifle shoved hard against his shoulder, and the limb splintered and fell.

Seldom's eyes flickered in surprise. "You ain't always been a farmer."

Daniel had, but he let the statement stand.

The Provost home was a big double log cabin. Aaron and Rebecca Provost had taken literally the Biblical injunction to be fruitful and multiply. Daniel was the eldest of a considerable brood, old enough now to take up his own land if ever he could raise the money it took to put in a claim.

Aaron Provost watched with interest by the open door of the long log barn. He stood six feet tall and more, shoulders broad, tough hands the size of a cured ham. He could lift a wagon while someone fitted a wheel, or he could throw a bull yearling to its side and hold it down by sheer muscle and weight. He could have broken a man's neck with one blow of a huge fist if he were so inclined, but Daniel had never seen his

12

father strike a man in anger. Provost was a friendly bear.

Aaron's eyes were boldly curious as he watched Milo Seldom, but he addressed himself to his son. "In early, ain't you, Daniel?"

"Brought a visitor for supper, Papa."

"So I see." Milo Seldom winced a little at the crush of Aaron Provost's hand; the big farmer didn't realize his own strength. "Name's Aaron Provost. You make yourself at home here, friend."

Seldom rubbed his throbbing hand. "Much obliged, Mister Provost. Brung meat for the table. Don't like to be a cost to nobody."

"A visitor's always a gain around here, not a cost. Daniel'll see after your stock, and I'll take you up to the house to meet Rebecca. She'll be tickled that there's somebody come."

Daniel asked Seldom, "Any special way I ought to handle them packs?" He hoped this would prompt Seldom to tell what was in them.

"Just throw them over the fence is all right. Nothin' there that can bust or leak out."

Aaron swung the deer carcass over his shoulder as if it had been a rabbit. He started walking toward the house with Seldom, but turned. "Daniel, you'll want to wash up and slick your hair before you come in. Lizbeth's here."

Daniel looked at the dusty patched clothes he wore and wished there were some way for him to change. But he owned only two pairs of britches and three

13

homespun shirts. Lizbeth Wills was used to seeing men come in from the fields; her father and brothers were farmers like the Provosts. And if she and Daniel married, this was the way she would see him the rest of her life. She had just as well get accustomed to it.

Normally the thought of Lizbeth being here would crowd everything else from his mind. It did something to him he never quite understood to put his arm around her when nobody was looking, and to feel the quick, shy response as she leaned to him. Sometimes she put something sweet-smelling on her neck—he never did know what it was—and it got him to breathing hard and thinking things he would be ashamed to tell her about. He was not naive; he knew exactly what this sort of thing eventually led to, though he had never so far let himself go beyond a furtive pinch or two where he had no business. Lizbeth always slapped his hand gently to let him know he shouldn't, but never stingingly enough to make him retreat altogether. She let him know without saying so that once the proper ceremonies had been attended to, he would be welcome.

The stranger was heavier on his mind now, however, than Lizbeth. Tomorrow Milo Seldom would ride out with hardly a backward glance, while Lizbeth would be here forever.

As he struggled to lift the heavy packs from the mules and hang them on the fence, he heard the girl's voice. "How do, Daniel."

Lizbeth Wills was tiny; he could almost reach

around her waist with his two hands. This had caused Rebecca Provost to worry aloud that she might not be strong enough to attend to all of a woman's work, though Daniel had noticed that the Mexican women of the Hernandez place upriver were small and seemed to have an unbounded capacity for labor. Daniel had never fancied the chunky or the big rawboned type of girls anyway; there were a few of them in the valley if his preference had run in that direction. Tiny or not, Lizbeth could cause him about all the excitement he was able to restrain.

Daniel glanced toward the house, saw nobody looking and gave her a quick promissory kiss. She touched him with both hands, then pulled back, remembering herself. "Supper'll be ready directly," she said. "Your mama is fryin' up venison from the deer the stranger brought in. I already helped with the bread." She was forever reminding him she could cook.

"What did you think of him, Lizbeth?"

"Not very fat, but he'll make passable venison."

"I don't mean the deer. I mean Milo Seldom."

She shrugged. "Never paid much attention to him. He's another rollin' stone without no moss on him. I like to see a little moss."

"Don't he make you itch to know the places he's been to, the things he's seen?"

"Why? I'm not interested in goin' anyplace. I like it here."

"Sure, this place is all right, but—" He broke off,

15

knowing he couldn't explain it to her. It was a woman's nature to be a nest-builder, to cling to what she knew. She couldn't know the way a man's eyes lifted to the horizons sometimes, the way a man's nature strained to shake the bonds and cross over the unknown hills. He said, "I'll go with you in a minute, soon's I get through here. Will you wait?"

"You know I'll always wait."

The children were noisy but the venison was good, and Rebecca Provost had fixed fresh bread from wheat Aaron Provost had carried way over east to the flour mill. Milo Seldom wolfed food as if he hadn't eaten in a week, and perhaps he hadn't. A drifting man usually carried coffee and salt and little else, depending upon game for whatever sustenance he got. But even venison cooked on a spit over an open fire could become tiresome after a while. A woman's touch was probably a treat indeed. Daniel noticed that Seldom gave Lizbeth much of his attention. Not that he tried to talk with her much; but simply that his eyes seemed always to stray back to her. Daniel supposed this ought to bother him, but somehow it didn't. It seemed confirmation of his own good judgment in latching onto Lizbeth himself.

Later, when supper was done and Aaron and Daniel and Seldom repaired outside to the brush arbor to cool themselves in the spring breeze, Seldom pointed his chin toward the door. "Mighty comely little girl, that one in yonder. She spoke for?"

Daniel shrugged. "Sort of."

"Smart of you, friend Daniel. A man needs a good woman if he's got him a place and goin' to stay put."

"Ain't got me a place of my own. Maybe someday, if I can raise the money."

Daniel's twelve-year-old brother Lod came out and flopped down on the ground to stare at the bewhiskered Milo Seldom in flagrant and unapologetic curiosity. Seldom commented that he looked nearly a grown man and won Lod's friendship for life. Then Seldom looked toward the cabin again. "Always wished for a little woman like that myself, only I'm always on the move, and a man can't ask a woman to follow along after him like a pet dog. Indian woman, maybe, or even a Mexican, but white women ain't made thataway. Sort of brings me up close and reminds me of my shortcomin's when I see a woman like yours. You're lucky."

Am I? Daniel asked himself. "Must be somethin' to get to come and go when and where you please, to stay where you want to, move on when the notion strikes you, to see new country all the time."

"The restless foot. I've always had it; been both a blessin' and a curse to me. A blessin' when I see somebody who's worked himself into the ground on one little place for years and got no more to show for it than I have. A curse when I see a pretty little woman and know I can't ever have one like her, just an occasional night or so of sinful pleasure in one of the settlements, bought the way a man buys a bar of lead or a little parcel of powder. But I can't change my ways;

17

they're settled too deep in me even if I wanted to get shed of them. Be content that you ain't got my rovin' nature, friend."

How do I know I haven't? Daniel asked himself. I've never tried.

Aaron Provost got out his old pipe and the leather pouch in which he carried his tobacco. Seldom blinked as if he had just thought of something. "Where'd you get the tobacco, Mister Provost?"

"San Felipe. Was down there on some land business with the guv'ment. Like to smoke?"

Seldom pushed to his feet. "Put it back in the pouch. I bet I got somethin' you'll like better." He strode to the barn. In a few minutes he was back, carrying a huge handful of leaf tobacco. "Try that. Bet you ain't had the like of this in years. Fine burley, prime stuff if prime was ever growed."

Aaron Provost smelled of it, and his mustache lifted in a broad smile. "I swum, lad, you are most certainly right." Eagerly he shredded tobacco for his pipe, lighted it and drew on it, eyes closed in pleasure. "Land o' Goshen, how this takes me back."

Daniel knew now the aroma he had smelled. "You mean that's what you got in them packs, is tobacco?"

"Not just tobacco, friend. Pure gold. I'm on my way down to Mexico to sell it. Them Mexicans will near give you gold ounce for ounce in trade for that kind of prime tobacco."

"I hear they got a mighty stiff tariff on it."

"Tariffs is for them that don't know the Mexican ways."

Daniel frowned. "You fixin' to smuggle it in?" He remembered an old rascal named Noonan who used to neighbor them here and who had told of smuggling tobacco into Mexico long before the big war with Santa Anna.

"Ain't nothin' sinful about a little smugglin'. Border lines is a thing of man, and contrary to all the laws of God and nature."

Aaron Provost's eyes were open again, and he was close to a frown. "There's talk we may be movin' toward another war with Mexico. You reckon a man ought to be goin' down there under them circumstances, sellin' stuff to people who may be fightin' us again one day?"

"I fought in the last war, Mister Provost, and if it comes to that, I'll fight in the next one. But maybe there don't need to be no war if people understand one another, and what's a better way to learn that than by trade? I say set up trade with a man and you don't have to war with him."

"Depends on how you trade," the farmer said.

Seldom shrugged. "Better tradin' than fightin'."

Daniel remembered what Seldom had said about standing on the threshold of wealth. Even granting that tobacco was worth a lot in Mexico, he couldn't see much wealth in three packs of burley. He said as much.

"The tobacco," Seldom responded, "is just the

startin' place. It's to give me money enough that I can go where the real riches are."

Little Lod asked, "And where is that?"

Aaron Provost admonished his son, "Another man's business is best left alone."

Milo Seldom studied the boy a while. "No harm done, Mister Provost. I see no reason I shouldn't tell you; there's no harm you good folks would do me. You remember Jim Bowie?"

"Him that died in the Alamo?" Aaron Provost looked over at Seldom. "He'll always be remembered in this part of the country."

"You ever heard about his lost silver mine?"

Daniel's backside began to prickle. "There was always talk that he found an old Spanish mine. Nobody ever knew where, or even if there was truth in it."

"He found it," Seldom said with confidence. "Way to the west, out in the middle of that Comanche and Lipan Apache country. Wasn't far from where the Spaniards built their fort on the San Saba and left it a long time ago. He found it, then he lost it. With what I get out of this tobacco, I'm goin' to go find it again."

Aaron Provost said soberly, "You'll find your grave, is all. There's Indians out yonder in that western country, thicker'n hair on a buffalo hide."

"But there's silver, too, and I'll have my share of that. Then the world will stop and tip its hat to Milo Seldom."

Daniel suspected nobody ever paid much attention to Seldom, and that probably rankled him. Come to think of it, he told himself, outside of family and a few friends there ain't nobody heard of Daniel Provost.

The women had come out into the cool and heard the last part. Rebecca Provost, a gaunt and patient woman, nodded knowingly, for she had heard many a dream spoken in words but had seen few lived out in deed. Lizbeth Wills listened with mouth open. She hadn't been around half as long as Rebecca.

Aaron Provost puffed contentedly on his pipe, enjoying the richness of the tobacco. "Every man to his own brand of religion I always say, and seekin' after riches is a religion to some. But the silver I want is right here on my own ground, in reach of my plow. It comes up fresh with every plantin' when the Lord sees fit to send the rain and withhold the pestilence."

Seldom replied, "And a good life it is too, brother, for them as has the gift to live it. But the Lord turned me another way, and who am I to deny Him?" He pushed to his feet. "I'll see after my stock before I roll out my beddin'. I'll want to rise early and be off in the cool of the mornin'."

Rebecca said, "Not without a good breakfast to give you strength."

"I wouldn't think of it, good lady. Cookin' such as yours is a blessin' that comes rare to a man of my nature." He bowed and walked to the barn.

"Strange man," Lizbeth said, watching with eyes showing awe. "Scares me a little."

21

"Nothin' strange about him," said Aaron, drawing on his pipe. "We seen a many like him back in Tennessee, and there's aplenty of them in Texas—backwoodsmen, men of restless foot, akin to the wild creatures that migrate with the seasons. There ain't no mystery to them; they're just men that ain't ever found their way."

"Idlers," said Rebecca. "Likeable, some of them, but idlers and misfits. They raise no crops, build no cabins. They move across the country like Indians. They contribute nothin' and leave no sign."

Aaron disagreed. "They contribute. They're the first ones into every new land. They're the ones that test the mettle of it and learn its ways. They open it up for the farmers and the others that set down roots. God made all kinds of men, and for every kind there's a reason."

Daniel's brow furrowed. "You reckon he *does* know how to find Jim Bowie's mine?"

Aaron shook his head. "A dream, that's all. But he knows how to hunt for it, and to some men the hunt is more important than the findin'."

2

INVITED TO SPEND THE NIGHT WITH THE PROVOST BOYS in the loft over the cabin's open dog run, Milo Seldom listened to the noise and politely declined, indicating he had rather sleep out by the barn than be a disturbance to anybody.

Lizbeth Wills stayed over and would sleep among the Provost girls, and as usual on such occasions, she and Daniel took a short walk hand in hand past the garden and down to the stock well and back toward the house. Also as usual, Lizbeth did all the talking. Most times Daniel would listen contentedly, enjoying the music of her voice and the exuberance of her dreams, but tonight he heard only a little of it here and there. His mind was on the stranger who rested out by the corrals; the stranger and the three packs of tobacco and the exciting times that must surely lie ahead of Milo Seldom.

Crisply, Lizbeth reproached Daniel for not listening to her. "Some other girl got you thinkin'?" she demanded.

"Been studyin' on that Milo Seldom, and the things he said. Been thinkin' what a farm I could buy if I had me a share of that Jim Bowie silver."

"He's crazy even talkin' about it and you're crazy listenin' to him."

"It's enough to set a man's mind a-runnin', all that silver out yonder waitin' for somebody."

"You'll find yours, Daniel, where your daddy found his—in the crops that come up out of your own ground."

"But that's painful slow. A man gets in a hurry sometimes."

Her tone softened. "I'm not impatient, Daniel; I ain't pushin' you."

"It's me that's impatient."

Her hand squeezed his fingers, and she leaned against him. "There's time."

When she stirred him like that, he didn't know if there was time or not.

It was customary for everybody to be up and about by first light, for the day was never long enough to do all the work that needed doing, but Daniel quietly climbed down from the loft even earlier than usual. He moved uncertainly toward the barn, half afraid Milo Seldom might have taken a wandering notion and be already gone. To his relief he saw the tobacco packs still slung across the fence, and the packmules and horse hobbled on grass, waiting time to be on the move.

Lod came trotting along barefoot, tugging at his britches. Daniel motioned for him to go back to the house, but Lod gave no sign he understood either word or gesture. Daniel decided to try to ignore him.

Milo Seldom was awake and dressed, if indeed he had ever taken his buckskins off. Daniel figured he probably had slept in everything except perhaps the heavy boots and the Mexican hat. "Mornin', brothers," Seldom greeted Daniel and Lod, sitting on his single blanket and scratching first his head, then his backside. "Womenfolks ain't already got breakfast, have they?"

It was still dark, and no candlelight yet showed through the open windows. "Not yet. They'll be up directly."

24

"Then I reckon I'll be packin' my mules and be ready. The early miles are the easiest. Late in the day a mile is hard won."

"I'll help you." Daniel took down a rawhide *reata* the Mexicans had taught him to use, for he suspected from the wild look that they carried about them Seldom's horse and mules might be mean to catch. But Seldom waved the rope aside. "I'd as leave not spoil them none. Feller uses the rope a few times, he can't catch them without it no more."

Seldom approached them with the bridle and halters, talking softly, reminding the animals of the biblical injunctions about hard work and faithfulness, and the penalties of sloth. In a minute he had all four properly caught and the hobbles removed. "When God gave man dominion over the beasts of the field, He meant him to use it with kindness," he told Daniel. One of the mules balked, so Seldom kicked it in the belly. "And firmness," he added.

Lod scurried around getting in the way, but Daniel knew something about packing mules and was able to help Seldom. He pointed this out in an oblique way. "I reckon it takes you awhile when you got no help."

"Time means mighty little to a mule."

"It can mean a right smart to a man."

"I trust the good Lord to give me time for what needs to be done."

The Lord gave Seldom time to put away breakfast the likes of which even big Aaron Provost seldom ate. When he was done and had wiped his sleeve across his mouth the last time, Seldom thanked the women for their kind attention and good cooking. Rebecca had made up some extra corn dodgers and put them in a sack. Daniel hoped Seldom would tie them where they wouldn't get taken up with the flavor of horse-sweat. Seldom said, "I'll remember you good folks when the weather turns cold and rainy, and it'll bring a little sunshine to warm my soul."

Daniel followed him out to the horse and the pack-mules, itching with the things he should already have said. "Mister Seldom, you'll be needin' help on this thing you're doin'."

Seldom frowned, sensing the rest of it. "I got some people down the way that I expect'll be willin' to go with me."

"You got one right here that's more than willin'."

Seldom looked him full in the eye, regret in his expression. "Been thinkin' you'd say that, and been wonderin' how I could answer you without causin' bad feelin's to either of us. You ain't the kind, Daniel. Maybe you think you are, but you ain't. You was born for farmin' and tendin' stock and for raisin' babies with some pretty little corn-fed girl like the one I seen here."

"Farmin' is not soft life; I know aplenty about hardship."

"But of another kind. A man can stand hardship when he's on land that he knows, when he's got his own people around him, when he knows where he's goin' to lay his head down come dark. It takes another

26

breed of man to stand hardship where he don't know no landmark, don't have no friend, don't know if he'll live to see the sun come up. I'd be doin' you a wrong in the eyes of the Lord was I to let you go with me and you not meant for the kind of trouble we'd ride into." He tried a weak smile that didn't work, and reached out to grip Daniel's hand. "You'd best stay home, friend Daniel. This is a growin' country. Texas need farmers a heap sight more than it needs tobacco merchants and treasure hunters. A man like me don't leave nothin' but tracks; a man like you leaves the land better than he found it."

Seldom gave Daniel no chance to argue. He swung easily up into the saddle, waved his hand in a broad motion meant for everybody, and rode away in a brisk trot, leading the Mexican mules.

Daniel's throat was tight with frustration as he watched Seldom move out across the rolling green prairie. At length he was aware of Lod standing beside him, eyes shining in admiration of Milo Seldom.

"You know somethin', Daniel?" Lod said. "When I'm old enough I'm goin' to get me a horse and some packmules and I'm just goin' to travel the country the way he does."

"The only mules you and me will ever handle is *plow* mules," Daniel said, a touch of bitterness in his voice. He turned away, knowing it was time to harness Hezekiah.

Daniel tried not to dwell upon his disappointment. He went to the field and attacked the plowing with an angry drive he hadn't had in a long time. The mule seemed to sense that he was not to be trifled with, for it stepped briskly and gee-hawed to every command. Daniel finished more plowing in less time than he had done all year.

He saw the mule's ears point forward and head go up in sudden interest, and he looked. Over the hill came two men on horseback, strangers.

Traffic has sure got heavy here of late, he thought, wiping sweat with his sleeve and licking dry lips as he thought of the water jug waiting in the shade. He finished the row and left Hez standing while he went for the water and waited for the men to reach him.

He decided right off that he didn't like their looks. Neither was inclined to show friendliness; if anything, they were suspicious.

"You!" one of the men said sharply. "Come here!"

He was a tall man in a badly worn beaver hat and a swallowtail coat which hung down on either side of the saddle. The command roused a stubborn streak in Daniel.

If he wants to talk, he'll have to come to me! He stayed where he was and took another drink from the jug. The men moved their horses into motion and came up to him. That gave Daniel a sense of satisfaction, a skirmish won.

The other man spoke next; a smaller, chunky fellow whose belly pushed against the front of the saddle. "We're lookin' for a man."

Daniel said, "Will I do? Name's Daniel Provost."

28

The tall man took it up impatiently. "Man we're lookin' for was leadin' three mules. Tracks show he come right by this field; I'd say from the sign that it was yesterday. Whichaway did he go from here?"

"You're friends of his, I reckon?" Daniel said innocently, knowing by the look of them that they were not.

The two men glanced at one another, the tall man scowling, the fat man snickering a little. The fat one said, "You could call us acquaintances. We're awful anxious to meet up with him again. Now tell us whichaway he went."

"What did he look like?"

The tall one said angrily, "There ain't been so many people by this direction but what you'd know the one we're talkin' about. He had three mules with him, and a pack on every mule. Now, we don't aim to be unfriendly about this thing, but we're askin' you one last time."

Daniel sensed threat about the two, not to himself but to Milo Seldom. He knew that lying about his having been here would do Seldom no good; if they had tracked him this far, they could track him more. "Yes, there was such man here. Come by late yesterday and asked if we'd feed him. Did he break the law?"

The fat one smiled without humor. "He done an unfriendly thing."

They know he's after the Bowie silver, Daniel decided, becoming increasingly concerned. They're

29

after it too. "Us Provosts don't hold with lawbreakers or shelter the criminal," he said. "If it was a thing like that, I'll tell you all I know about him."

The fat one said, "All you got to do is tell us which-away he went, when he left here. That'll gain us time we'd otherwise lose followin' tracks."

"West," Daniel lied, "toward Austin town, where they're buildin' the capitol. Said it would be a good place to sell some tobacco."

The two men looked at each other, then stared at Daniel. He stared back, trying to keep his face from betraying him. He felt no guilt, so he knew there was no reason for his face to give him away. The tall man gritted, "If you was to lie to us, we'd take that as an unfriendly thing."

"I don't know you or him either. Why should I lie?"

"He's got an easy way with people; they'll always lie for him."

The fat one nodded. "Come along, Bodine. We're keepin' a farmer from the tillin' of his fields."

The tall Bodine grumbled under his breath as they rode away. He kept looking back, but to Daniel's satisfaction they rode west. They had taken his word—maybe. But they probably wouldn't take it for long. When they had ridden awhile and hadn't cut any sign of a trail, they would probably come back. What they might do then he didn't know.

What he *did* know was that he had to warn Milo Seldom. He itched to be about it immediately, but he held himself in check, knowing they might be suspicious, knowing they might be watching. He had to go back to his work and give them time to decide he had told them the truth. It was hard going, plowing the length of that field, then back again, itching to be on his way but fearing to move from the job at hand.

By the time he had made it back to the starting point, he could not hold himself any longer. He unhitched Hezekiah from the plow, jumped up on the mule's back and bare-heeled him into a reluctant trot, then finally into a rough lope toward the house.

He picked up his roan horse Sam Houston grazing the green grass and hazed him into a pen. Not pausing to unharness Hezekiah, Daniel bridled Houston and threw his saddle up onto the horse's back.

Lod trotted barefoot from a garden where his father had left him hoeing. "What's the matter, Daniel? You see Indians?" His voice was hopeful.

"Not Indians. There's a couple of hard-lookin' fellers after Milo Seldom. I sent them the wrong way, but they'll be onto me soon enough."

"I'll go with you."

"Like hell you will! You'll slip the harness off of Hezekiah and see that he gets somethin' to eat." Lod opened his mouth in protest, but Daniel cut him short with an angry glance. "You argue with me and I'll wear a hole in your britches with a harness strap! Do what I tell you now, and keep out of my way!"

Daniel led the roan out and, swinging into the saddle, loped him toward the house. His mother looked up in surprise from the fireplace as he burst through the door. "Land sakes, where you goin' in such a hurry?"

"Maybe to Mexico; I don't know." He grabbed his old longrifle from its pegs on the wall, and the powderhorn and shot pouch that went with it. Face stunned, his mother demanded to know what the matter was.

"Got to go help Milo Seldom," he blurted. "Lod can tell you."

"Son—" She tried to grab him. He gave her a kiss and was gone before her hands could clasp him and hold him back.

"Mama, if I don't come back awhile, you'll know I went with Milo. Tell Lizbeth so she won't worry."

"So *she* won't worry?"

She followed him, throwing out questions so rapidly that he couldn't have answered them even if he had been so inclined. "*Adiós,* Mama," he shouted back at her as he quickly mounted, the powderhorn swinging wide from his shoulder. He pulled the roan around and set him quickly into a run, wishing he had spurs. That was something that as a farmer he had had no reason to buy or have made for him. He swung around the garden and the near cornpatch, and then he was on his way south as hard as he could push the roan.

He knew the trail Milo Seldom had taken, for it led by the Hernandez place and ultimately joined with other trails that eventually would take a traveler into San Antonio de Bexar. Nearly every trail into Mexico went one way or another by San Antonio, for this ancient town had been the heart of Mexican Texas, pumping the lifeblood that had kept it alive for almost a century and a half under the flags first of Spain, then of Mexico. When a traveler skirted around San Antonio there was usually a reason, and not an honorable one. Daniel saw no reason why Milo Seldom should want to avoid town.

He found a horse and three mules no problem to track, especially since they stayed on the trail; the sign was plentiful. Daniel pushed the roan as much as he dared, loping him awhile, then slowing him to a trot to keep from breaking him down. The trot kept him impatient, and in a short while he jumped the roan into a run again.

Finally, ahead of him, he saw the man and the mules. Shouting and waving his hat, Daniel tried to get Seldom's attention. If Seldom saw him, he gave no sign.

If I was an Indian, Daniel thought, I could kill him and he'd never know what hit him.

Milo Seldom dropped out of sight over a hill. Frustrated, Daniel kept heeling the roan.

Two men burst out of a thicket and stopped their horses in the trail directly in front of him. Too late, Daniel tried to rein around them. His roan bumped one of the horses, and Daniel almost went down. When he grabbed Houston's mane and pulled himself back into the saddle, he was staring into the awesome bore of a rifle that looked like a San Jacinto cannon.

"Now, farmer," the fat man said, that mirthless smile cutting across his face again, "I'm purely disappointed in you. If ol' Bodine here wasn't of a suspicious nature, we'd probably be halfways to Austin now. Always been my misfortune that I trusted people too much, and often as not they've cashed me in. Now, you wasn't figurin' on goin' on down yonder and tellin' Milo Seldom we was comin', was you?"

It was a useless question not meant to be answered. Daniel's throat was dry all the way down. The longer he looked at that rifle, the bigger it got.

"Farmer," the tall man growled in evil temper, "if there was any profit to be got out of it, I'd shoot you. I might decide to do it anyway just to see whichaway you fall."

"Now, Bodine," said the bewhiskered fat one, "he wouldn't be of no earthly use to us thataway. Besides, folks around here might get fussy over a man shootin' a farmer, though Lord knows the country's purely overrun with them these days. No, seems to me like ol' Milo might be tickled to see this friend of his. Might be glad to treat with us, knowin' we wouldn't shy from takin' desperate measures." He glanced at Daniel and added, "If we was forced to it."

Daniel tried to swallow, but his throat was shut.

Lanky Bodine said, "You know that shootin' eye of Milo's. If he was to take the notion, he could pot you quick as we come in sight. Time I could get to him, he could be reloaded and get me too."

"How do you know I'd be the one he'd shoot first?"

"You're the broadest target. A man like Milo who's been hungry all his life just mortally hates a fat man anyhow. Smart thing for us to do is to take this farmer and follow along and keep out of sight. First time he stops, we'll work around him and get ahead. Then we'll step out and surprise him as he comes up on us."

It seemed to Daniel that if Milo Seldom had even one eye open or his ears weren't plugged with dirt, he ought to be able to see or hear them going around him and be on the *cuidado*. He made it a point to hit the hard ground where he could, for the hoofbeats drummed louder there, and he popped brush when it came handy. If Milo Seldom was half the frontiersman he appeared to be, he would end up doing the trapping rather than being trapped.

It was all for nothing. Bodine and his fat partner set up position in a motte beside the trail. Bodine kept the long barrel of his rifle pointed at Daniel's head. "Now, farmer, don't you even breathe loud."

Daniel hardly breathed at all.

Milo Seldom came along directly, head down and whistling a tuneless ditty. If thirty war-painted Comanches had been astraddle the trail, he would not have seen them.

The fat man eased out of the motte, and Bodine followed, silently motioning for Daniel to do likewise. "Well now, Milo, ain't this a pleasant surprise?"

Milo Seldom stared in astonishment. He never made an effort to lift the rifle from his lap. He swallowed and finally said, "Naw, Fanch, it ain't overly pleasant."

Fanch grinned. "Depends mostly on which side you look at it from. Me and Bodine, we're mighty pleased about the whole thing. See you taken good care of our mules."

"They *was* your mules. They been mine the last several days."

"We're mighty glad you got the use of them, Milo, but now we're takin' possession again. We hope you got no strong objections."

"I sure do."

"They as strong as ol' Bodine's rifle that he's got pointed at your farmer friend? Or as strong as this Jim Bowie frogs-ticker I got here in my hand?" Fanch waved his big Bowie knife and passed it so near to Seldom's throat that Seldom could almost taste the forged steel. Seldom shook his head in resignation. "Naw, they ain't that strong."

Fanch said, "Many a thing I don't like about you, Milo, but one thing a man's got to give you credit for: you're reasonable."

Daniel decided they weren't going to hurt him or Seldom; if that had been their intention, they would have done it by now and not wasted all the talk. He could see that Seldom was losing the mules and their burden, and with them the dreams of the silver mine. Daniel's fear subsided, and anger rose in its place. He was angrier at Seldom than at Bodine and Fanch. He said critically, "If you'd been payin' attention, you wouldn't of let yourself get caught thisaway. I done everything but set off a cannon."

Seldom made no effort to reply; he looked like a dog that had been given a couple of licks with the double of a rope.

Fanch said, "You'll find that's somethin' else about Milo; he ain't dependable. He's a dandy at hatchin' up schemes but mighty slack at seein' them through. Careless is what he is." He reached for Seldom's rifle.

Bodine still had his own rifle pointed at Daniel. "You'll have to get off of that horse, farmer. We got to take your horse to keep you from any notion of fol-lowin' after us. A little walk back to the farm will give you plenty of time to consider your follies."

"You got no right to take my horse."

"We'll turn him loose down the trail someplace. If he decides to come home, fine. If he don't, maybe you can get Milo to work it out." He poked at Daniel with the rifle. "Now git on down."

A clatter of hoofs came from atop the hill, and a rattle of chain. And down rode Lod Provost heeling the plow mule Hezekiah, the plow harness still on him. Bodine turned in surprise and let the rifle sag. Daniel grabbed it and pushed it away from him, trying to twist it from the tall man's hands. Instinctively Bodine pulled the trigger. The big blast went off close to Daniel's ear, though the ball passed harmlessly by.

The suddenness of it spooked Daniel's horse, and he plunged forward into Bodine's. Off balance, Daniel sailed out over the horse's neck and straight into the tall man. Together they went over the rump of Bodine's startled mount, which kicked and wheeled away. Bodine hit the ground, Daniel on top of him. Something snapped. Bodine howled in pain.

"My arm! Damn you, farmer, you done busted my arm!"

Daniel desperately grabbed Bodine's rifle by its hot barrel, not realizing for a moment that it was useless until he took time to reload it. No, not useless; it would make an awesome club. A rifle barrel heavy as that could brain a man.

He thought then of Fanch and the Bowie knife and spun around, the rifle over his shoulder and ready to swing in self-defense. He held it that way, for in the moment of confusion Seldom had come into possession of the knife, and the situation had reversed itself. "Now, Fanch," Seldom said quietly, the point of the blade at Fanch's belly, "you just hold yourself real still. I always had an evil temptation to slice a fat man open and see if anything besides grease would spill out. Don't do nothin' foolish that might help Satan overcome my Christian nature."

Bodine squirmed on the ground. "My arm! My God, ain't nobody goin' to pay attention to my broken arm?"

Seldom showed no concern. "Which arm is it, Bodine?" He looked for himself, and seemed disappointed. "His left one. Friend Daniel, you ought to've broke his right arm instead; that's the one he shoots with."

Daniel momentarily turned his attention to his

younger brother, sitting on the lathered mule. "Lod, what the devil you mean followin' after me thataway? I told you to stay home."

Lod ignored the question. "How come you to bust that feller's arm?"

"Lod, it's a wonder you didn't kill that poor ol' mule, runnin' him thataway. Now you get yourself home and tell the folks I'm goin' on with Mister Seldom."

Milo Seldom blinked. "I don't remember sayin' nothin' of that kind."

"It's plain to me that you need help, even if you don't see it. I can at least keep you from ridin' off into a ditch or somethin'."

Bodine kept crying about his arm. Seldom paid no attention to him. "Well, you did show a right smart of gumption toward these two evildoers."

Lod Provost asked, "Daniel, how come you broke that feller's arm?"

Seldom finally gave some attention to Bodine, who sat in the trail holding the arm and hollering. "Fanch, you git down there and see if you can't do somethin' that'll shut him up. I swear, there ain't nothin' gets my hide to crawlin' like listenin' to a growed man cry."

Daniel sent Lod to catch his and Bodine's horses. Daniel's rifle was still tied to Bodine's saddle.

Not trusting Fanch with the knife, Seldom cut the sleeve from Bodine's dirty homespun shirt. The arm was crooked, all right. Seldom put his foot against Bodine's shoulder and pulled the arm. Bodine bawled and fainted. Seldom said, "I believe I got the bone set,

39

Fanch. You find a stick and use that sleeve to wrap it around his arm."

Bodine came back to consciousness, groaning and acting grievously sinned against. Fanch said, "You got any whisky, Milo? It'd sure help him with his miseries."

"A clear head will let him contemplate his sins and help him decide to set his feet aright upon the path to glory. And now it's time for me to be settin' *my* feet upon the path to San Antonio. I swear, interruptions like this sure do slow a man up."

Daniel said, "You didn't say yet, Milo, if I'm goin' with you."

"I thought *you* had already said it. Come along; you've earned a share."

"I ain't got no money with me, not a dollar, not a peso."

"Who *has,* this day and time?" Milo swung into the saddle and took up the lead line for the pack-laden Mexican mules. "Catch Bodine's and Fanch's horses, will you, Daniel? Them two boys won't cause us no worry if they ain't mounted."

The fat Fanch was sweating. "You ain't stealin' our horses and settin' us afoot out here, are you, Milo?"

"Not stealin'. Like Bodine told my friend awhile ago, we'll turn the horses loose someplace down the way. If they decide to come back to you, that's just fine. If they don't, you'll find walkin' is good for your wind."

"But Bodine's got a broken arm."

"He ain't goin' to walk on his arm."

"You goin' to leave us our guns though, ain't you? Else how'll we eat?"

"Use a snare, Fanch. You and Bodine, you always been good with snares of one kind and another."

Daniel told Lod again to go home. He wanted to see his brother well on the road before he left these men here. He didn't want them catching up to Lod and taking the mule away from him. Lod said, "What'm I goin' to tell Pa? He's apt to be a little pouty; the plowin' ain't finished yet."

"Tell him when I come home I'll finish it with a *silver* plow."

"Lizbeth, she ain't goin' to be overly happy either."

"She'll have silver rings for her fingers."

Lod nodded. As he turned to leave, he said, "You never did tell me how come you to bust that feller's arm."

"Go home, Lod." Daniel watched his brother ride over the hill and wondered what tangled tale he would tell when he got there.

Fanch stood glumly watching, hands clasped under his sagging belly as Seldom and Daniel rode off, leading the packmules and the two men's horses. Bodine sat in the trail, long legs stretched out in front of him, splinted arm hanging in a sling made from the other sleeve. He was hoarsely crying something about having pity on a poor, crippled old man.

Daniel rode a long time in silence, quietly studying the calm countenance of Milo Seldom. Seldom

41

seemed unshaken. Looking at him, a stranger would not know he had been through anything more eventful than stopping to fix dinner.

At length Daniel asked suspiciously, "What's that they said about these bein' their mules? And it was their tobacco, too, I reckon."

"All in how you look at it. They'd stole it all off of somebody."

"How'd you happen to come by it?"

"We had us a little game of cards."

"Way you talk, I wouldn't think you'd hold with gamblin'."

"I don't. But when I play cards it ain't gamblin'. I was taught by masters."

"You mean you cheat?"

"Now, *cheat's* a strong word. I just take all the opportunities the good Lord sees fit to offer me. I don't ever play against a righteous man. I play only agin the evildoer."

"I don't see where that makes it any better."

"Anything I get takes it out of the hands of the unrighteous and robs the devil of his due. Them two, Bodine and Fanch, they'd of just sold that tobacco and spent the money on spiritous liquors and lewd women and such. I intend to use that money in ways pleasin' in the sight of the Lord."

"Such as?"

"I don't rightly know yet. I'll study on it."

3

MUCH OF HIS LIFE DANIEL PROVOST HAD HEARD men speak in hushed tones of San Antonio de Bexar as if it were some sacred city. Perhaps in a way it was, for many men had shed their blood here in the name of their country, whether Texas or Mexico or Spain. He would not have been surprised to see roofs of shining silver and streets of gold. Instead he saw a motley scattering of rock and adobe structures small in size and indifferent in flat-roofed architecture. Dust curled in the streets as the wind sought its way past battle-gutted houses that had never been rebuilt. Standing much taller than the one-story buildings was a single church tower somewhere toward the center of town.

Daniel stared in awe at a collection of two-story ruins surrounded by a half-ruined rock wall. Before Seldom told him, he already knew what it was.

"The Alamo," Seldom said. "A hundred and eighty men, *mas o menos,* lie buried over yonder—what was left of them after Santa Anna had the bodies burnt." The crumbled walls were half overgrown with weeds, and the facade of what had once been a stone chapel was pockmarked by cannon balls and smoke-darkened from fire and shell. Chills played down Daniel's back.

"I'd like to go over and take a closer look," he said.

"Did you have somebody die in the Alamo?"

Daniel considered himself a Texan, the name given to those settlers already here when the war was fought. "A hundred and eighty men."

"There was a time before the war when this town must of had seven-eight thousand people. You'd have to scratch now to turn up a thousand. I doubt as San Antonio will ever amount to anything any more. Or Houston, either. You watch—these wide-awake towns like San Felipe and Harrisburg will take it all away from them."

They crossed the clear-running San Antonio River, which Seldom said was fed by springs above the city. Daniel had noticed many Mexican dams and ditch systems or *acequias* carrying water to fields and gardens. Cattle and sheep wandered unattended, grazing at will on the property of all who had not bothered to put up fences. A wonderful place for lawyers, Daniel judged.

He was disappointed at the extent of abandonment he saw here, rock and adobe houses crumbling away, roofs caved in either from cannon fire or from neglect. Even many of the standing buildings bore deep scars. At least three times in a decade this city had seen bloody turmoil. Farther back, when Mexico had won its independence from Spain, the city had violently changed ownership more than once. And when settlers and soldiers were not fighting one another, there had been the Comanches. At times they had seemed to consider this city their own private hunting preserve. They had stalked stragglers at its fringes and more than once had boldly raided along its streets.

"An unhappy place when you come down to it," Seldom commented. "Twenty years from now there won't nobody even remember this town, and a good thing that'll be."

They rode along the river in the waning daylight. Daniel saw some young Mexican girls bathing openly in the clear water, splashing and giggling, innocent of any clothing whatsoever. He turned away in shock but was compelled to look again.

"We can join them if you'd like to," said Seldom. "We could use a little washin'."

Daniel shook his head, his voice lost. He felt guilty staring at the girls because the thought came unbidden that this was how Lizbeth must look undressed. He felt as if in so thinking he had somehow violated her virtue. Just the same, he kept looking.

Seldom volunteered, "Place we're goin' to is a little farther up the river. This is where we'll join up with ol' Cephus Carmody. He's the man who can lead us to the silver."

They came at length to a small adobe house surrounded by a crude picket-type fence built of mesquite limbs, raw-hided tightly together and stood on end, reinforced by a row of heavy cedar posts standing ten or twelve feet apart. "Cephus' place," Seldom said and waved for Daniel to follow him through the open gate.

A slender girl knelt at the edge of the river, rinsing clothing and beating it against a rock. A big pile of wet

45

clothes lay beside her. Daniel thought she glanced back once, though he wasn't sure.

Milo Seldom stepped down and dropped the reins. He walked up behind the kneeling girl, swung his hand and gave her a smart slap on the rump. "Howdy, Flor."

She came up from her knees and whirled to face him. In one single unbroken motion she brought up the flat of her hand and fetched him a slap that sent him staggering back, a flash of red fingermarks on his cheek. He raised his hand in surprise and rubbed his stinging face.

"Wait a minute, Flor; it's me, ol' Milo."

"I know damn well it's you, Milo Seldom," she stormed, "and you're makin' mighty free with your hand. One of these days I'll take me a knife and cut it off for you one finger at a time!"

Daniel stared openmouthed. From her appearance he had taken this to be a Mexican girl, though her voice carried only a hint of accent, not nearly so much as the Hernandez girls had back home.

Seldom remonstrated, "Now, Flor, I got me a friend here. What's he goin' to think, hearin' that kind of language comin' from such a pretty girl?"

The girl's dark eyes fastened briefly on Daniel Provost, giving him a quick appraisal and coming up with a negative reaction. "If he's runnin' with you, Milo Seldom, I'll wager he's seen and heard a damn sight worse. Now, I've heard you say howdy. Let's hear you say *adiós*."

46

"I've hardly just come."

"You could've not come at all and I'd be happier."

"My friend Daniel is goin' to get the notion you ain't in love with me."

"If he's smart at all, he's done figured that out. Though if he was very smart, he wouldn't be with you in the first place."

Seldom watched the girl warily, trying to pass over her hostility as if it were nothing. "Flor Carmody, this here is Daniel Provost. He's a farmer from up the country aways. He done me a good turn, and I've made him a partner in a venture. We're here to see your daddy."

Flor Carmody shrugged. "What do you want with that old sonofabitch?"

Daniel spoke Spanish, and he knew that *flor* meant flower. Whoever had named this girl had been overly optimistic.

Milo said reproachfully, "The Good Book tells us we should honor our father and our mother."

"I honor the memory of my mother. My father never had any honor."

"He's bound to've had some, Flor. He married your mother."

"Barely in time. My grandfather and my uncles had a lot to do with that."

Milo dropped the argument. "I sure do need to see ol' Cephus. Where's he at?"

"In Mexico. Some damned *Americano* of about his own stripe came by a few months ago and they went

47

off to smuggle goods across the river."

Crestfallen, Seldom seemed to try to find a reason not to believe her. "I can't picture ol' Cephus runnin' off and leavin' you here by yourself."

"Why not? He's done it aplenty of times. I take care of myself."

It dawned on Daniel then why she was washing so many clothes. Seldom nodded his chin at the pile and said, "You makin' your livin' like that?"

Flor Carmody picked up a wet black dress and held it in front of her. It was twice her size. She snapped, "You can tell it's not mine."

"Looks to me like there ought to be an easier way."

"There's one," she gritted.

Seldom stared, suddenly alarmed. "Don't even joke about a thing like that."

"I ain't jokin'. I just ain't got that hungry yet."

"Maybe we could find you somethin' better than washin' out other people's dirty clothes, else you'll be an old woman before your time. Maybe we could find somebody willin' to marry you."

She doubled her fist as if to swing at him. "Milo . . . ."

He backed off, putting up his hands. "I swear, girl, I don't see why you always got to be so hostile this-away. I never done you a bad turn in my life."

"Like hell you haven't!" Slowly she loosened her fist. "It's no use. You're what you are and don't even realize there's anything wrong with you. It's your nature and I reckon you couldn't do anything about it if you wanted to. It's just that you're so much like the old man—rest-

48

less as a cat and about as responsible. He wore my mother out tryin' to follow him; she's buried God knows where along some damn horsetrail between here and San Felipe. He's wore two more women since, to where one quit him and the other one died. I swore when I got old enough to make my own livin' that I wouldn't follow him no more, and I don't."

"You don't have to take it out on *me*. I ain't in no way responsible for what Cephus has done, and I sure ain't ever asked you to marry me."

"No, Milo, you haven't. A better man might've."

"You'd of turned me down."

"If I'd had any sense."

"One thing I got to say about you, Flor, is that you've always had good sense. No manners at all, but plenty of sense."

"I'm fixin' to show my bad manners and ask you-all to leave. I got work to do."

Milo seemed not to hear. "Flor, I got to find ol' Cephus. It's important."

"Nothin' you or him ever did was important."

"This is. This time we're goin' after ol' Jim Bowie's silver."

She brought her hands to her hips and stared at him in contempt. "You and the old man have been talkin' about that silver for years, sayin' you'd go after it soon's you had the money to hire the men and buy horses and mules. You'll never live that long; neither one of you could ever hold onto a coin."

"I got the money."

She snorted. "I'll believe it when I can count it in my hands."

"Well, I ain't exactly got the cash, but what I got here'll bring me the cash."

She looked at the three pack-laden mules and shook her head, more in pity than derision. "Most people do their dreamin' when they're asleep."

"I got three packs stuffed full of prime tobacco. You know how them Mexicans like good tobacco, and how they'll pay for it."

"And you know what they'll do when they catch you smugglin'."

"They've never caught me yet; well, not but once or twice. When this is over I'll be richer than the king of Sheba."

"That's *queen* of Sheba. And if I remember my readin', she finally got snakebit."

Daniel had read a little history and knew they were both wrong, but he had read enough human nature to know this bout was deeper than any question of historical kings and queens; something strongly personal went back a long way with these two.

Milo shook his head. "No snake's goin' to bite me this time; I got the good Lord on my side."

"He's been on your side all along or you'd been killed in some folly years ago. How'd you come by them mules and that tobacco anyway? I'll take a vow that you never done no work for them."

"The Lord provides for them that watches out for theirselves."

50

"Good thing he watches out for you, too."

"You got to help me locate Cephus."

Her sarcasm was strong. "Split that silver with me?"

"I'll bring you ten times the clothes you got layin' there. They'll all be yours, too."

She told him Cephus Carmody had teamed with an old bandit named Notchy O'Dowd out of his own native Redlands, that stretch of unpoliced outlaw country that lay between the western settlements of Louisiana and the easternmost of Texas. Mexico imposed a high tariff on imports of foreign merchandise, and there was such a strong demand for such goods that a man with a little daring could make himself a small fortune if he remained uncaught. Cephus Carmody had been smuggling goods since the filibustering days long before Stephen F. Austin had set up his first American colonies in Mexican Texas. He had guided a couple of ill-fated Texan expeditions to invade Mexico, these excursions failing because of Texan exuberance and underestimation of the enemy rather than any shortcomings on the part of the guide. Cephus Carmody had made a lot of money in his time, and spent it faster than he made it. One day silk, next day patches.

"That's where you'll find him, is in Mexico. Last I heard, the town of Colmena Vieja."

"Then that's where we'll go, is Colmena." Milo walked back to one of the mules and began to untie the pack. Daniel, who had sat on his horse and listened all this time, did likewise.

Flor Carmody demanded, "What do you think you're doin' now?"

"We'll stay in San Antonio a while, at least till tomorrow. Got to rest up the stock. You got some grain around here, ain't you?" He didn't wait for her answer. "I thought I'd try to find a couple more good men to go with us. You know if Lalo Talavera and Paley Northcutt are around anywheres?"

"Birds of a feather!" she said sharply. "You'll find Lalo wherever the most women are at. Paley Northcutt'll either be in jail or just gettin' out or puttin' himself in a fix to get back in. Try the *calabozo* first and then the *cantinas* and the alleys. You know all the places."

"I swear, Flor, you are the most cuttin' woman." Milo slipped the pack off one mule and hoisted it with heavy effort onto his shoulder. He carried it toward the rock house.

Flor took a few steps away from the riverbank and demanded, "Where you goin' with them packs?"

"Puttin' them in the house. You don't think I want to get all this money rained on, do you? Come on, friend Daniel, we got some huntin' to do."

She ran ahead to the door and blocked it, eyes blazing. "That's *my* house."

"Sure it is," Seldom said soothingly. "You think we'd leave this stuff with somebody we didn't trust?" He pushed past her, dumped that pack and went back for another. Flor Carmody watched in silent anger.

Daniel felt sorry about the way Milo Seldom was

putting upon her. "Ma'am, I sure hope we ain't bein' no bother."

Her eyes cut right through him. "Now that," she jabbed, "is even dumber than anything *he* said."

Daniel retreated to the horses. Flower, he thought, mulling over her name. They ought to've named her Cactus; they'd of been closer to the truth of it.

Seldom turned the mules into a mesquite-limb pen and fed them grain he found in a rawhide-and-willow barrel. He walked to his bay horse and swung into the saddle.

Flor Carmody shook her fist at him. "Milo Seldom, you come back here and take your mules and your packs with you. I don't want them."

Milo smiled and started riding away. "We'll be back tonight, Flor. Don't you be waitin' up for us."

She cursed him in bristling Spanish till they rode out of earshot. Seldom said, "She speaks both languages, one as good as the other. Her mother was Mexican." He smiled, satisfied with himself. "You wouldn't think so, but that girl's been in love with me for years."

"It'd be easy to fool somebody."

"I might even let her marry me someday, if my foot quits itchin'. Man needs a gentle little woman to take the rough edges off of him and help him find the Lord's true pathway to peace."

4

THOUGH IT HAD DWINDLED TO A THOUSAND PEOPLE, San Antonio was the biggest town Daniel had seen. He stared in awe at the mass of rock and adobe houses which in many cases stood wall to wall, more like prison compounds in appearance than like individual homes. Whatever yard they had was in the back. A person who stepped out of his front door was immediately in the street and in some hazard of being run over by a passing wagon or wooden-wheeled *carreta* if he was not on the *cuidado*. The danger was not great, however, for the traffic moved at a leisurely pace; tomorrow was time enough for a task not finished today, and if not tomorrow, then the day after.

Many of the houses were deserted and caving in, but as Daniel and Seldom rode toward the heart of the city, he saw that the larger percentage there were lived in. The streets in the cool of the late afternoon were increasingly coming alive with horses and burros, dogs and children. A sow and her pigs rooted in a muddy hole left by a recent rain, and scrawny chickens scratched for bits of grain in the dried droppings of animals.

Seldom pointed. "Ol' Paley Northcutt used to live over thisaway."

"That girl made out that he's somethin' of a drinker."

"Paley has pulled a few stoppers in his day. The

Lord gives most every man a weakness to test him. But you get Paley away from the big city, away from the demon spirits, and he's as good a man as it ever pleasured you to ride with. Got nerve like a Mexican cougar."

He stopped in front of an adobe house where a sagging wooden door stood open, and a tiny brown-skinned girl stared big-eyed at the two *extranjeros* on horseback. She was clad in nothing but a curious expression. "*Chiquita,*" Seldom asked, "*donde está tu mamá?*"

A Mexican woman stepped into the open doorway, a baby clasped against her ample breasts, her long black hair hanging in wild disarray. Seldom bowed in his saddle and swept his hat from his head. Daniel hurried to copy him. Seldom said in as florid a Spanish as Daniel had ever heard, "Ah, *señora,* you look as beautiful as ever. The years touch on your features as lightly as the passing shadow of the dove in flight."

She was unimpressed. She answered crisply, "If you seek the *Americano* Northcutt, who is totally without value and should be cast naked among the wolves, he is not here."

"Where then might he be?"

"In prison, if justice were truly done, though there is no justice in this city under *Americano* rule, or *Tejano.* When last I saw him he owed me four month's rent. I chastised him with a broom and sent him fleeing like a whipped dog into the street."

55

That, Daniel thought, ill fitted the image of the cougar.

Seldom gave her mild reproach. "To sleep in the mud, with the cold rain beating down upon him and the bite of the night air chilling his poor tired bones? Woman, is there no charity in your heart to match the beauty I see in your face?"

"It would be a charity to this good city if the Northcutt were to die in a drunken stupor, or drown in a goatskin of *pulque. Adiós, señor.*"

"*Adiós,* fair lady of the flowers." Milo Seldom pulled the bay horse around and shrugged at Daniel. "Don't fret, good friend, we'll find him."

If Daniel fretted, it was over the possibility that they might. "I never heard Spanish as pretty as that. Where'd you learn it?"

"From Lalo Talavera. A better hand with the ladies you'll seldom see."

They rode through the heart of the city, which lay a little to the west of the Alamo ruins. Daniel marveled at the size of the big stone church which stood on the main plaza, and at the long rambling structure which had been the palace of the Spanish governors and later the Mexican officials who had overseen this part of Mexico until brutal Santa Anna discarded Mexico's constitution and threw Texas away in an ill-managed campaign to drive the *Americano* settlers back across the Sabine.

Seldom said, "It was right here in these streets that the idea first come to Jim Bowie about the silver mine."

56

"How?"

"Them Lipan Apaches, they used to come into San Antonio to trade for goods. They'd always bring silver with them. Now, silver didn't mean much to an Indian except for the ornaments he could make out of it, but he learned quick that it meant somethin' to the white man, and that he could trade it for things that meant somethin' to him, like powder and lead, and cloth and such like. Well, the Mexicans in San Antonio tried at first to trail them Indians and find out where the silver come from. Some of them never come back; most of them just lost the Indians somewhere out yonder to the wet and come draggin' in afoot and hungry. Time come when the Mexicans quit worryin' about it and took it for granted.

"But you've heard stories about Bowie; he wasn't no man to pass up a chance at treasure. The kind of life he'd lived, he'd charge the fires of hell with a bucketful of water. A man who'll let them nail his britches to a log and set there and fight a knife duel with somebody else nailed down the same way—he ain't goin' to let a few feathers scare him. He wanted that silver, and he set out to get it. But he was smoother'n a card player about it and took his time.

"He made friends with them Indians; they could tell he wasn't no ordinary man—he was somebody come. He got to goin' west and tradin' with them and huntin' buffalo with them and all. Lived amongst them awhile, even, all the time keepin' his eyes open. And finally one of them Indians showed Bowie where the silver was at. Now, the way it was told to me, it was out yonder close to the old San Saba mission. Them Spaniards had them a silver mine, workin' it with Indian slaves. Come a time finally when the other Indians killed a lot of the Spaniards and run the rest of them off. They left silver bullion that they had smelted but didn't have no chance to carry away. Ain't no tellin' how much—thousands of dollars' worth, maybe, or hundreds of thousands, or millions. *Quién sabe?*

"Now, Bowie knowed that Indian shouldn't of showed him the place; soon's the other Indians found out, they'd kill them both. So Bowie took note of where it was at, then he got his horse and he rode for San Antonio as hard as he could go, movin' like the devil beatin' tanbark. He got him up a party of men, a dozen or more, with plenty of horses and guns, and they went back to find that mine.

"When they got near the place they found Indians, dozens of them, and hostile to the bone. Them treasure hunters, they had to fort up in a big live-oak motte. When the battle was over, there was dead Indians scattered up and down the creek but a lot more live ones still rarin' to fight. In the end there wasn't nothin' for the bunch to do but retreat. They come back to San Antonio badly whupped. Jim Bowie always said he was goin' back, but what with one thing and another he never did get another party together. Then come the war, and the Alamo. I wonder sometimes if he died thinkin' of all that silver that he never did get ahold of."

Daniel said, "Bowie's long dead. What makes you think that after all these years we can find the mine?"

"Bowie's dead, but not all the men that went with him out to the San Saba. There's a few that outlived the war. I got one who says he seen the mine with his own eyes, and he's been waitin' for years till we could get men and guns and stock enough to go."

Daniel felt his heart quicken. "Cephus Carmody?"

"The same."

"He's sure he can go back and find it after all this time?"

"A thing like a mine full of silver a man ain't goin' to forget. Sure, he'll find it for us. We'll all be rich, friend Daniel. The Lord will open up his bounty and bless us like kings of old. But first we got to have the men." He pointed. "There's a couple dozen *cantinas* where we might find Paley, but the easier thing might be to find Lalo Talavera first. Maybe Lalo'll know where Paley is at. They run together now and again. Over thisaway used to be a lively Spanish girl that Lalo had eyes for."

In a few minutes they sat their horses before a stone house, somewhat more substantial and better kept than the adobe where they had sought Northcutt. Seldom said, "I could get interested in this girl myself if ol' Lalo didn't have a prior claim." He dismounted and drummed his knuckles against the wooden door framing. As before, he bowed and swept his hat gallantly at the appearance of a strikingly handsome young woman. "*Señorita,* my eyes are dazzled by the

59

brilliance of your smile. Each day that passes makes you more beautiful. I am seeking our mutual good friend Lalo Talavera. I know he has never been able to remove himself far from your beauty, and I thought by chance he might be here now."

A man's voice replied from inside the room, and an angry-faced young Mexican pushed himself in front of the woman. "He is not here. If ever he comes here again, he will be dead in a moment, as you will be, *señor,* if you do not leave this place immediately."

The woman said shakily, "My husband, sir."

"And my error," said Seldom, bowing again but pulling back toward the horse as he did so. "Surely I have mistakenly come to the wrong house. My apologies." He moved quickly away, glancing once over his shoulder as the man and woman disappeared back into the room's darkness. Shaken, he said, "Like to've turned over the whole pot of beans there. Reckon the best bet now is to look in on the *fandangos* tonight. Lalo has an eye for women and an ear for music."

A feeling of mutual suspicion still persisted between the Mexican majority in San Antonio and the American minority, though the war had been several years ago and though most of the Mexican people still here had taken no strong side in it one way or the other; the ones who had given heavy support to Santa Anna had mostly fled after his defeat. And there were some in San Antonio such as the powerful Seguin family who had fought beside the Texans against the man they considered a tyrant.

Despite the suspicion, friendships had grown between individual Mexicans and individual Americans. Daniel noticed that Milo Seldom had friends here, drawn to him perhaps because they were somewhat kindred in spirit, taking today for the pleasure that was in it and letting tomorrow's troubles await the sunrise of another day.

Seldom made the rounds of friends' houses, greeting the men with the *abrazo* and the women with a high-blown line of exaggeration. He and Daniel visited in the city awhile, then at the suggestion of one of Seldom's friends rode out to the edge of town to one of the many *ranchos* clustered there within reach of mutual protection should Indians strike. Around these *ranchos* grazed uncounted Mexican ponies and mules. Seldom tried to talk first one friend then another into selling him horses on credit. But there was a point at which friendship ended. When finally they accepted an invitation to a supper of goat meat and beans and flat *tortillas* of pounded corn at an adobe ranchhouse a couple of miles from the city, Seldom still had not talked anyone out of a single animal.

"A tribute to their business judgment but a poor reflection of Christian generosity," Seldom complained.

At full dark he and Daniel rode once more down the narrow, dusty streets. Fiddle music rose on the night air. It came from several places. "Now maybe we'll find of Lalo and Paley," said Seldom. "This is when they shine the brightest, after the moon is up."

61

Daniel had never been to a true Mexican *baile* or dance, so the first one held considerable interest for him. He and Seldom followed the fiddle sound to a stone building perhaps thirty feet long. He had to duck just a little to pass through the door, for the Mexican people were generally of smaller stature. The women and girls were mostly seated on benches lined along the sides of the room, and the men were either standing or walking around, talking to each other or to the girls. The arrival of two *Americanos* attracted momentary interest and suspicion, for some of the rowdier of the blue-eyed breed had been known to descend *en masse* upon such a gathering, throw out the men and take charge of the womenfolk. But some of the people here recognized Milo Seldom and pronounced him harmless.

Daniel noticed a couple of the handsome girls staring at him and whispering to each other, hiding all but their eyes behind their fans. The attention made him self-conscious and ill at ease, but not so much that he was ready to leave when Seldom told him Lalo Talavera was not here.

"Let's stay and watch a few minutes," Daniel said. The fiddle struck up a Mexican waltz, and the floor quickly had all the couples who could conveniently dance in the limited space. Daniel tapped his toes and watched the swirling feet, trying without much luck to pick up the secret of the step. It went too fast for him. He wanted to ask one of the girls to dance and see if he could master the waltz; he also wanted to see if these girls would feel as good in his arms as Lizbeth. But he didn't muster the nerve. It might be easier, he thought, fighting Indians.

At length Seldom took him out, assuring him there would be other *bailes* down the street, even better ones. They visited a couple more *fandango* places and still didn't see Talavera. "Maybe a little early for him," Seldom mused. "He might be otherwise occupied."

He had heard there was to be a *maromeros* show of rope dancers and actors in a nearby courtyard, and suggested that perhaps Lalo might turn up there. They went to a place where a couple of fires had been built in a large private yard to provide light for the show. Daniel watched with interest the rope dancing and the acrobats' tumbling. A couple of the older Mexicans complained that it was being clumsily and amateurishly done by this younger generation, but to Daniel who had never seen anything like it, it was a grand show. Then a handful of actors and actresses put on a couple of farcical skits so earthy in the visual aspects and so explicit in the Spanish language that Daniel found himself blushing in the darkness. He looked about, puzzling at the complacent attitude of the women in the audience. He had not thought women ever heard such words or even knew their meaning.

Lalo Talavera did not appear. Daniel could tell Seldom was becoming impatient. They left the firelight and started walking up a dark narrow street.

Seldom was saying, "We better find them before the sun comes up, or they'll both take to the shade where they can't be seen."

Daniel heard what he took to be a groan and, catching Seldom's arm, silently pointed. The sound came again, only this time it was more a belch, then a short siege of coughing.

Seldom slapped Daniel on the back. "Luck's with us, Daniel; I'd know that belch in the devil's own bar-room."

Paley Northcutt lay on his back, sprawled half in and half out of an open doorway, a jug of *tequila* strangle-gripped in his right hand. Daniel could smell him easier than he could see him in the dark shadows of the moonlight. Paley hadn't shaved in a long time, and his whiskers were long and matted; he hadn't bathed for even longer, Daniel judged.

Seldom crouched over his old friend, who lay in a stupor, totally oblivious to everything around him. Seldom said, "My, Paley, but you're a sight for sore eyes."

They'd have to be awful sore, Daniel thought.

"Well," Seldom said, "at least we know where he's at. We can come back and get him later; he won't be goin' noplace."

It was Daniel's judgment that Northcutt wouldn't be going anywhere for a long time, unless somebody carried him.

"Still a couple of dances we ain't been to," Seldom said. "If we don't find Lalo there, we'll start over. If he's in town and ain't got a broken leg, he'll probably show up."

They visited another dance place, and Daniel saw as pretty a set of dark-brown eyes there as he had ever seen. The girl all but asked him aloud to dance with her, and Daniel brought himself to take the bait. He bowed from the waist and asked her in the best Spanish he knew. She curtsied and came into his arms and the fiddles struck up a fast one. For a moment Daniel gave himself to the intoxication of the girl in his arms, the sweet smell of whatever she had put on herself. He fancied this could have been one of the girls he had observed earlier in the afternoon, bathing in the river.

The step became too fast and intricate for him, and he found himself stepping on her feet as she gamely tried to set him aright without taking the lead herself. He spun and spun with her, and almost lost his footing. Daniel decided it would be wise to admit the music had beaten him and make as graceful a retreat as possible under the circumstances. The girl tried to keep her composure and held a forced smile, but he could tell she was relieved when he led her off the floor and back to her place on the bench. It would probably be a while before her eyes flashed invitation to another clumsy *Americano*. Chagrined, Daniel jerked his head at Seldom to let him know he wanted to leave.

"They'll respect you for tryin'," Seldom said.

"But laugh at me just the same."

"Probably you was meant for the fields and the prairies, not for the dance floor. Dancin' is an instrument of the devil anyway, arousin' fires between man and woman and leadin' to all manner of sin." He walked along in the darkness, keeping his head cocked to one side, listening. "Bothers me that we ain't seen Lalo. He's one of the most popular men in town."

At this moment they heard another fiddle and Seldom said, "That'll be a place we ain't looked yet." The fiddle stopped before they could locate it, and for a moment they were at a loss as to where the music had come from. Then they heard a woman's scream and several excited shouts. Seldom began to trot. Rounding a corner, they saw people spilling out of a candlelit stone house.

Seldom stopped at the door and looked in. From his expression revealed by the candlelight, Daniel could tell he was suddenly disturbed. "Lalo," Seldom said beneath his breath and stepped through the door.

A handsome young Mexican stood with back to the far wall, his face twisted in desperation. Facing him were three other men, two carrying knives which they held outthrust, one toward the man's throat and the other toward his belly. At a glance Daniel knew they were about to use them.

Seldom did not hesitate. He strode across the room and shouted, pointing his finger at Lalo Talavera. "There he is, Daniel. That's him, the *cabrón* who has been after my wife!"

The Mexicans turned to stare at him in astonishment. None seemed more astonished than Lalo Talavera, whose eyes stayed open wide right up to the instant Seldom's hard-swung fist landed squarely between them. Seldom's other fist drove into Talavera's flat belly. As Talavera sagged forward, Seldom caught him, hoisted him neatly up over his shoulder and turned belligerently on the men who stood there.

"I've found him, and don't none of you try to help him! He's got a good stompin' comin' to him, and by the Eternal, I'm the one that's a-fixin' to give it! I'm sorry if I've went and disturbed the *baile*. You-all go right on with your dance; I'll take care of this outside."

Before the men were over their surprise, Seldom had toted Lalo into the darkness. Looking back over his shoulder, he carried him around the corner, then began to trot, bent under the heavy burden. Daniel followed, keeping a watchful eye behind them. If there was pursuit—which he doubted—it was quickly lost in the dark.

In a few moments they reached the bank of the narrow San Antonio River. Seldom walked into it, unceremoniously dumped Talavera and came back to dry ground. He squatted and watched Talavera sputter and thresh. The Mexican crawled part way out on hands and knees, threatening all manner of reprisal.

Seldom said calmly, "Better speak soft, Lalo, else

you'll draw them boys with the knives down here. What was they, jealous husbands?"

Talavera, still on all fours, wiped a wet sleeve over his face and stared at Seldom. "Milo, it is you?"

"Anybody else ever hit you thataway?"

Talavera watched him a moment, as if trying to decide whether to laugh or fight. He chose to laugh. "One was a husband. A mistaken one, of course."

"Of course." Seldom looked at him quietly. "But them boys was fixin' to dice you up or make jerky of you. If you had any brains, you'd stay out of other men's yards and not provoke them thataway. There's aplenty of girls that ain't married."

"One tries to work where one is most appreciated." Lalo rubbed a hand cautiously over the bridge of his nose and flinched. "One eye will surely be black tomorrow. And I think my nose may be broken."

"Didn't help my hand none either. You got a hard head." He rubbed his knuckles ruefully. "When you get through wadin' out there, Lalo, come along with us. We got places to go."

Lalo Talavera came out of the river, the water streaming from his clothes. "Go? Go where?"

Milo Seldom explained briefly that they were leaving in the morning for Mexico, there to sell his tobacco and finance their trip west to search for the lost mine on the San Saba. "It's the big chance we've talked about for so long, Lalo. I'm offerin' you the opportunity to go and earn a share of all that silver."

Lalo whistled under his breath. "The many times we

have talked, I have never thought it would ever happen. It is a thing to dream of, like marrying the beautiful daughter of the governor of Coahuila. A share, you say? A full share?"

"A full share. Everybody that goes gets an even share. Since I'm furnishin' the stock and the supplies, my even share is bigger than the others."

"How can they be even shares when some are more even than others?"

Seldom looked at him a moment, then at Daniel. "I hadn't thought on it thataway. We'll work it out." He told Talavera that they had located Paley Northcutt and would go pick him up. "We got the goods at Flor Carmody's place. That's where we'll leave from."

"Ah, *sí* the pretty Flor. A lovely flower to behold."

Seldom's eyes narrowed. "That's one flower you'll leave alone, Lalo. Any pickin' to be done there, I'll do it."

Talavera smiled. "That proud beauty will have none of us, you *or* me. She has a wish for better things."

"And what's the matter with *me?*" Seldom demanded.

"Nothing, old *compadre,* nothing. I am but remarking upon the foolishness of women."

"Well, it's time we went and got some rest; that's why the Lord gave us the night. Comin', Lalo?"

"In the morning. I will be there by the first light. But for now, I must go and have my wounds bound up."

"What wounds? Any little scratch you got, I can fix it."

"But not with the gentle hands and soft manner of one I know."

"If she's got a husband, you better leave her alone. You won't be much use with a knife in you."

Daniel and Seldom went back to the dark street where they had found Paley Northcutt. So far as Daniel could tell, the man hadn't wiggled a finger; he lay there just as he had before. Seldom picked him up and hoisted him onto his shoulder.

Daniel suggested, "Couldn't we dump him in the river like you done Talavera? He could sure stand the bath."

"It wouldn't keep. Give him a week or two and he'd be the same again."

Daniel hoped Seldom would make it all the way back to the Carmody house with his burden, but he didn't, and Daniel had to carry the man awhile. He kept his head turned to one side and breathed through his mouth.

At the Carmody house they found the tobacco packs all lying out in the open yard. Flor Carmody came to the door when she heard them. She was dressed in some flimsy shift for sleeping. Even if scandalized, Daniel still could not help but stare. Seldom said, "Flor, we put that tobacco in the house to keep it safe."

"You think I want this house smellin' like tobacco for six months? I drug it back outside and there it's goin' to stay. You try to move it in here again and I'll shoot you in the foot. That's where all your brains are."

"I swear, Flor, you can be the most unreasonin' woman."

"You've seen only my good side." The wooden door closed, and Daniel heard a bar fall into place.

Seldom muttered the Lord's name in vain. "Sometimes I don't see why He didn't let Adam alone and leave that rib where it was."

Daniel eased Northcutt to the ground and laid his head on a tobacco pack, trying to make him comfortable. On second thought he doubted it would make much difference; in his condition Northcutt could sleep on a rock pile.

Seldom said, "A thing like this needs guardin', Daniel. Me and you'll take turns. You stand the first watch and I'll stand the next. Wake me up in about two hours."

Daniel sat on one of the packs, rifle close at hand, and watched Seldom fall quickly into a sound sleep. In the distance he could still hear the sound of a fiddle, and he thought of that dark-eyed girl whose feet he had so clumsily abused. He guessed that was something he would tell Lizbeth about sometime, though it might be wise to keep it to himself. She might take it as disloyalty, his wanting to dance with some other girl so soon after leaving her. She wouldn't understand how he could be attracted by some other woman's flashing eyes; he didn't entirely understand it himself. But he found himself thinking more about that Mexican girl than about Lizbeth; perhaps there was something to the saying that a man's eyes began to wander when *he* did.

He stared awhile at Milo Seldom, and at the unconscious Paley Northcutt. Maybe Milo knew what he was doing, but Northcutt and Talavera seemed an unlikely choice for a trip like this. For that matter, he had some doubts about Milo Seldom.

At length he judged that the time had passed, though he had no watch to go by. He shook Seldom's shoulder and roused him. Seldom yawned and scratched and raised himself up, looking around as if unsure for a moment where he was.

"Your time to guard the packs," Daniel reminded him.

"Oh, yes, almost forgot. You get yourself some sleep, friend Daniel. We'll travel aways tomorrow."

Daniel stretched out on his blanket. The last thing he saw before he drifted off to sleep was Milo Seldom, sitting on a pack and yawning.

Sometime later—he couldn't judge how long—a mutter of voices awakened him. He started to turn over and felt something cold press against the back of his ear.

"Just you move nice and easy, farmer boy," a rough voice said. "Don't do nothin' that'd give us cause to burn powder on you."

Daniel turned over carefully, suddenly wide-awake and knowing that what he had felt was the muzzle of a rifle. The first thing he saw was Milo Seldom, lying against a pack and not fully awake. Raising his eyes, Daniel then saw four or five men standing in the moonlight, all carrying rifles or Mexican *escopetas*. The one nearest Daniel had his arm bound up. This was the gaunt Bodine.

Bodine said, "You-all raise yourselves up slow and careful. We've done took over."

72

5

DANIEL GOT TO HIS FEET, NO SLEEP LEFT IN HIM. HE counted four men, Fanch, Bodine and a pair whom he took in the moonlight to be Mexicans. Milo Seldom was still blinking; he hadn't quite comprehended it all yet.

Daniel felt like hitting him. "You-all got no right. This tobacco belongs to Seldom."

"Well now," grinned Fanch, slouching back on his heels so that his belly seemed to stand out even farther, "first it was ours, then it was his, now it's ours again. Only thing a man can be sure of in this world is change."

Daniel wondered if they knew about Seldom's idea for going after Bowie's silver. Surely Seldom wouldn't have been dullard enough to have let them hear of it; no, on second thought, maybe he would.

One of the Mexicans who had only a knife nudged Paley Northcutt with his toe. Northcutt hadn't made any response to the command, and the Mexican wanted to know what was the matter with him. Seldom said, "He'll do you no harm. He's had a little to drink."

"That," said Fanch, "is the one thing you've ever said that I would believe." He surveyed the packs, kicking at one of them with a booted foot. "Looks like our merchandise is still all here, Bodine."

"You got no right," Daniel said again.

73

Bodine thrust the muzzle of the rifle forward. "Farmer, you better put a hobble on your lip. I ain't forgot who it was broke my arm."

The one-handed way Bodine held that rifle made it probable that the recoil would break his other arm if he fired it. But from the direction in which it was pointed, Daniel wouldn't have lived to enjoy the satisfaction.

Seldom said, "I wouldn't provoke them none, Daniel."

Daniel turned his anger on Seldom. "Damn you, Milo, you went to sleep. If you'd been on guard, they wouldn't of slipped up on us thisaway."

He might have predicted Seldom's reply. "Like the Book says, the spirit was willin' but the flesh was weak."

Daniel had heard about all the biblical quotations he was interested in for a while. He cut loose with a vehemence that comes by nature to a man accustomed to dealing with mules.

Head down, Seldom said quietly, "It grieves me to hear such language spill from the lips of one I took for a Christian."

"And I took *you* for a frontiersman. All you are is talk!"

The exchange pleased Fanch. He moved in closer like a better at a cockpit. "Go after him, farmer boy. Eat him up!"

Fanch wasn't as careful as he should have been, either. He stepped between Daniel and the other three men and let his rifle barrel dip in his enthusiasm for the verbal hiding Daniel was giving Milo Seldom. Daniel saw a chance to grab the fat man, wrest the rifle from him and use him as a shield to force the others back. He swung both hands down and got a grip on the rifle, then twisted suddenly and started to bring the muzzle up in an arc that turned it away from him.

That was the moment Paley Northcutt chose to turn over; he bumped against Daniel's leg. Daniel staggered, losing his footing. He saw Bodine's rifle barrel come swinging at him and was powerless to get out of its way. His head exploded and he felt himself fall back across Northcutt. Someone stepped on his belly and took most of the breath out of him. He saw nothing but bright flashes whirling behind his eyes.

He heard Fanch say, "No, Bodine, ain't no call for killin' him."

"I ought to," Bodine growled, "for what he done to me."

Milo Seldom wasn't saying a thing. He just stood there, hands about half up. He made no move toward Daniel because any suspicious move on his part might draw a rifle ball. At length he said, "Kind of a surprise, Fanch, you-all showin' up. Didn't figger to see you again."

"Bet you didn't," replied Fanch. "But the Almighty must be smilin' on us because you hadn't been gone hardly no time till a couple of Mexican travelers come along. We took the borry of their horses and rode off down the trail to where we found our own that you had turned loose. When we got here we found a few friends and done some askin' around. Wasn't no trick to find you, Milo. Ain't hard to outguess a man who's set in his ways."

Bodine pointed his chin suspiciously at the rock house. "We better take us a look in yonder."

One of the Mexicans said in Spanish, "It is where the girl lives, the prideful halfbreed."

"We better get her out here where we can watch her. If she's half Mexican, she's probably got a knife." He motioned for the man to follow him and went to the door. He found it barred. "Open up in there. Open up, I say!" When nothing happened, he had the Mexican try it with his shoulder. The door still held. Bodine said, "Bust in one of them windows."

There was no glass in Flor Carmody's house, or in most others around. The windows were nothing more than small wooden doors hinged to swing in and fixed so they could be barred. The Mexican threw his weight against the wooden window until finally the bar snapped and the window flew open. He leaned inside for a glance around. "Too late, *hombre.* There is a window in the back also, and the little bird has flown away."

Bodine shrugged. "If she's gone, she can't be stickin' no knife in my back. Let's get them packs loaded."

Daniel had lost a great deal of interest in the whole affair; his head throbbed so much that it was hard to keep up with anything else. He found warm blood

76

beginning to stiffen his hair. He wished he was home.

But he *wasn't* home, and he could see the rogues forcing Milo Seldom to saddle his horse and Daniel's as well. Daniel wondered vaguely where Fanch and Bodine planned to take them, though he hurt too much to care.

The mules were quickly packed. Fanch said with obvious relish, "All right, Milo, you and the farmer git into your saddles. No use lettin' this fine night air go to waste."

Milo gave no argument and Daniel couldn't. It was all he could do to grope his way to the horse and find the stirrup with his foot. His head felt as if an axe were splitting it when he put his weight onto the stirrup foot and swung up. He almost fell over the other side.

Milo said, "Daniel is in no condition to ride."

Bodine gritted, "I wasn't in no condition to walk, neither, but you left me afoot."

"I'll be havin' to hold him in the saddle," Milo grumbled.

"No you won't," said Fanch. "You'll be too busy holdin' this other one here." He motioned to the Mexicans and they lifted the drunken Paley Northcutt up behind Milo's saddle, leaving him lying with head down on one side, feet on the other.

"You," Milo said, "are the cruelest of Philistines."

Fanch smiled. "We try not to do a job halfways and leave it."

They rode out of the yard, Fanch's and Bodine's rifles pointing the way. Daniel couldn't see much of the path they followed, but he could see the rifles well enough.

Fanch and Bodine soon reined up. Seldom had one hand entirely occupied keeping the occasionally struggling Northcutt from slipping off onto the ground. Sooner or later the jouncing on his stomach would have to bring up the *pulque* or *tequila* or whatever it was he had been drinking.

Fanch said, "Well, Milo, this here is where us and you part company. Miguel and Paco here are goin' to take you-all for a pleasant ride in the country. A nice long ride, so lean back and enjoy it. Any scenery you miss on the way out, you can get a good look at on the way back. You'll be walkin'."

Milo said, "I done insult to the Philistines. You-all are worse."

"You try to remember that," Bodine replied, and he pulled away. Fanch followed him, leading the mules.

One of the Mexicans motioned with his rifle. "There will be time enough for talk as you walk back. Right now you will ride and be quiet."

They rode silently for a long time. Finally Seldom said, "At least they don't figure on killin' us."

"Don't they?" Daniel said painfully. "It's killin' *me*."

It wasn't doing Paley Northcutt much good, either. They had to stop eventually to let him rid himself of a night's indiscretions; when he was done he was more or less awake but deathly sick. The Mexicans showed him little patience. They prodded him to his feet and made him get astride the horse behind Milo. A couple of times he slid off, so Milo had to put Northcutt in the saddle; Milo rode behind the saddle and held the man to keep him from hitting the ground again.

Daniel moved in something of a daze; the wound had long since stopped bleeding, but he could feel dried blood matted in his hair. They hadn't picked up his hat for him; it still lay in the yard at Flor's. He would miss it when morning came and the sun came up. Things would get worse before they got better—a lot worse. He wondered if that gun barrel had cracked his skull. He guessed it hadn't, or he wouldn't be here.

He had no idea where they were going, not even the direction, for when he tried to look up and find familiar stars the pain would grab him and he had to let his chin sag. He knew only that they were in rough hills, where big live oaks stood tall and awesomely dark in the light of the moon. One Mexican rode in the lead, the other in the rear. They had the thing figured out pretty well. Daniel was too numb to make a move against them, and Milo Seldom had his hands full keeping Paley Northcutt on the horse. In his own way Northcutt was in as much or more pain than Daniel; another time, Daniel might have felt sorry for him, if he hadn't felt so sorry for himself. Northcutt was a totally innocent victim; he had joined Milo Seldom without even being aware of it. Daniel, at least, could not make that claim.

Sunrise was beginning when the Mexican in front

drew rein. "This," he said in Spanish, "would be a good place to die."

Daniel swallowed, not really believing. In Paley Northcutt's face he saw an expression almost of hope; Northcutt was so sick that death would come like a friend bearing money from home.

Milo Seldom argued with the lead Mexican. "Now, I know ol' Fanch well enough that I'm fair certain he didn't tell you to kill us. Stomp on us a little, maybe, but not kill us."

A mocking smile touched the Mexican's face; to him it was a joke. "Bodine said we should kill you. But the Fanch he said that would be a poor way to end a long friendship. He said you left him to walk; now we are to leave you to walk. It is a long way back to San Antonio de Bexar. If you move with diligence, you should be there by tonight. By then the last of the tobacco money will have been spent on *pulque* and *tequila* and the bright-eyed women with fire in their blood." He took the reins from Seldom's and Daniel's hands and nodded his chin in a way that said he did not care if all the *Americanos* killed each other. "If ever you get back to the city, seek me out. I have an uncle who is a good maker of shoes." He paused, the smile fading. "But come in peace, for I have another uncle who is an undertaker. *Adiós, mis amigos.*"

The two men rode away leading the horses. Daniel Provost found a fallen live-oak trunk and sat down. Paley Northcutt sprawled out belly down on the green grass. Milo Seldom just stood and watched until the horses and riders were out of sight. When he turned he was not so much angry as sad. "Good Lord only knows when I'll ever get a chance again at Jim Bowie's lost silver."

As far as Daniel was concerned, that silver was no more lost than *he* was, and he said so. Seldom shrugged. "No trouble gettin' to town, except it'll take us awhile. Yonderway's San Antonio." He pointed. But watching the sun come up, he was taken by doubt. "I could be mistaken, maybe it's a little more in that direction."

Daniel looked at the ground, disgusted, but seeing no gain in showing it. Maybe it was a good thing it had turned out this way; Seldom probably would have taken them off into Indian country and gotten them lost. It would probably have been their luck to ride into a Comanche campground and be guests of honor at a scalp dance.

To his credit, Milo Seldom showed concern for Paley Northcutt. He knelt by the suffering man. "You all right, Paley?"

Northcutt tried to heave but had nothing left to lose. He said, "I feel like I been hit in the face with the afterbirth of a buzzard."

Daniel thought he smelled like it, too.

Northcutt got up finally into a sitting position. Through the flushed red of his eyes there peered an incongruous touch of curiosity. "Milo, I been scratchin' my head and doin' my damndest to remember, and still it don't come to me what the hell

I'm out here for. Last thing I remember I was sittin' in an alley with a jug in my hand. Did I do somethin' foolish?"

"It's a long story, Paley." Milo looked back to where he thought San Antonio was. "I'll tell you sometime when I feel better myself. Right now we'd as well be a-walkin'."

Milo Seldom, bearing neither wound nor sour stomach, struck out in the lead, setting a pace that quickly proved too much for the other two men. Paley Northcutt staggered, fell and pushed to his knees. Milo Seldom said, "Maybe this will be a lesson to you, friend Paley; the worst miseries that flesh is heir to is the ones that go down the throat."

Northcutt managed to get to his feet again. He staggered along, stubbornness and anger keeping him going. Not very peart himself, Daniel began to admire the man's determination. His admiration was not that strong, however, that he let himself get downwind of him.

At length they came to a stream, and Daniel asked which one it was. He could see worry in Seldom's face; though Seldom quickly gave a name, Daniel suspected he had arbitrarily picked one.

Paley Northcutt waded out into the water and began bringing it up to his dry lips in cupped hands, trying to put out a fire in his belly. He lost his footing and fell threshing, going under once, coming up shouting for help and going under a second time. Daniel waded toward him, but Seldom said, "Water ain't over his hips if he ever finds his feet. The bath'll do him good."

Daniel considered that a moment; the idea had some obvious merit. But he had heard of a drunk drowning in a foot of water, so he grabbed the man under the arms and brought him to his feet. Northcutt pawed and choked and sputtered. He blinked, trying to get the water out of his eyes, but it kept running in from his hair that lay plastered across his forehead.

"Be easy, Mister Northcutt," Daniel said, holding the man's arm. "You'll be all right directly." He led the man across the shallow stream and up the opposite bank. Northcutt sat gagging. "I swear, if the good Lord meant a man to drink that much water, he'd of made him a duck."

Whatever else it had done, the stream had washed some of the stench from him. And once he was over the near-strangling, he seemed stronger than before; he stood steadier, walked easier. Daniel had taken a good soaking himself and felt better for it, though his head still ached as if someone had kept striking him with the flat edge of a Mexican sword.

They walked on through the morning, pausing now and again to rest. Northcutt began to complain of being hungry. No telling how long since he had last put a good meal under his belt. Now that the liquor was wearing off, he had nothing left to keep him going.

Seldom said, "It's a good sign, you feelin' the pangs like that. I been seein' some bees. I expect there's a bee tree around here close." While Northcutt and

Daniel sat down, he went out to look around. Daniel had noted long ago that some backwoodsmen had a second sense when it came to finding honey caches. He supposed that living on little but wild meat most of the time gave them a craving.

It wasn't long before Seldom hallooed from a couple of hundred yards away and indicated he had found the tree. When Daniel walked over to help, Seldom sent him back. "I don't want you to angry up the bees. I got a way with them; they don't ever give me no trouble."

Daniel walked back to Northcutt and sat down. Presently he saw Seldom begin to dance and swing his arms excitedly, then break into a hard run toward the creek. Even at that distance his shouts of pain came strong and clear, and the names he used in vain had not all come out of the Bible. He dived into the water and stayed there.

Daniel and Northcutt waited awhile, giving the bees plenty of time to get over their mad and be on about their business. Seldom waded out of the water, face swelling angrily in several places. "Paley, I don't want to hear no more about your stomach. I'll be lucky if my eyes don't swell to where I can't even see."

Daniel couldn't resist asking him what had happened to his easy way with bees. "Bound to've been somebody messin' with them; got them all spoiled and suspicious," Milo replied.

Sometime after the sun had started its afternoon

slant, Milo commented that he was having trouble seeing through his swollen eyes. "Boys, I can't say I'm right sure where we're at."

Daniel thought that had been the case even before the incident with the bees, but he had had no inclination toward mutiny. He studied Milo. "No disrespect, Mister Seldom, but I'm powerful disappointed in you."

"It was them bees that throwed me off. I think now that San Antonio is yonderway."

Paley Northcutt squinted. His eyes were dull and tired, but the sickness was gone. "I say you're wrong, Milo. I say Bexar lies in that direction." He pointed differently.

Daniel listened to them argue until he tired of it, then decided to try his own instincts. "I got a notion it's thataway," he said, pointing in a third direction, "and that's the way I'm goin'. You-all try your own ideas, and whichever one of us makes it into San Antonio will try to borrow some horses and come back lookin' for the others."

He struck out walking. Presently he looked back and found both men following him.

Well, he thought, it ain't the first time the blind led the blind.

In normal circumstances it would have gratified him to have other men follow him, but this time he had no particular faith in his own ability to find the way; the fact that they fell in behind him simply revealed they had no faith in their own. The more he thought about it, the more dismal the prospect became. On top of the pain and the weariness, he began to be aware that his stomach was empty. They had not even the makings of a snare, and it was obvious they wouldn't try to rob any more bee trees. Well, they would do the best they could; precious little edge they had for doing otherwise.

It seemed to him they had walked three times as far as they had ridden through the night, though he guessed that was an exaggeration. The sun bore down heavily upon his bare head, and the heat and the wound together brought nausea. It was as bad when he stopped as when he walked, so he kept walking each time until his legs caved, pausing then to rest and let the other two catch up with him. It surprised him that despite his condition he seemed always to be out ahead of them. It didn't occur to him at the time that they might simply be letting him take the responsibility for the direction so that if it turned out wrong, they wouldn't share the blame for it.

Afternoon wore into evening, and evening into night. He had a thirst that water wouldn't slake; he suspected he was running a fever. He dragged one foot dully past the other and somehow kept himself moving. He no longer looked back to see if Seldom and Northcutt were following him. If they were, fine; if they weren't, the hell with it.

He came finally upon a narrow trace that appeared to have been used by the high-wheeled Mexican *carretas*, though not enough to have worn it deeply. In this part of the country all trails led to San Antonio. Or *away* from it. In this case he couldn't tell which. He looked back for counsel and saw the two men too far behind him for consultation; they wouldn't know anyhow, he decided. He picked a direction and moved on. Seldom and Northcutt followed him.

He was about to quit and lie down on the bare ground for a night's fitful sleep when he saw flickering lights ahead. Blinking, he made out the glow of lanterns and candles, tiny and elusive spots of yellow in the night. He said in relief, "San Antonio. I'd about give up."

Seldom wheezed, "I knowed you was goin' right. If you hadn't been, I'd of corrected you."

It was still a long way into the city, but he found strength he didn't know he still had, and he plodded along doggedly ahead of the other men. By now he knew the dark streets well enough to have no trouble finding Flor Carmody's place. He walked past barking dogs and idly curious loungers and came up finally into the open yard of the little rock house on the river. He saw the girl standing there, and three or four men with her, shadowy figures in the moonlight. It came to him that they might be Fanch and Bodine for all he could see. He was too bone-tired to know or to care.

Flor walked out and stared at him a moment; he sagged, but he kept his feet. "Where's the rest of them?" she asked. Too weary to speak, he jerked his thumb. Flor said with a hint of respect, "Outwalked them, did you? Better man than I took you for. Don't reckon you've had a lick to eat?" He could only shake his head. "Come on in and I'll get you some *frijolis and tortillas*. It's the best I can do."

Beans sounded good to him. She paused long enough to tell one of the men—all were Mexican—to watch for Milo Seldom and Paley Northcutt. One of the Mexicans trailed in after him, and he recognized Lalo Talavera. Daniel was in too much distress to worry whether Lalo had been here paying court to Flor despite what Seldom had told him.

Flor gave Daniel a jug of *pulque* and told him to take a long drink. "It'll help you more right now than anything else you could take," she said. When he tilted his head up with the jug, she saw for the first time the ragged wound across his scalp. She held the candle closer and swore in unabashed Spanish. "You walked all day with that, and bareheaded? You *are* a better man than I gave you credit for."

By the time Seldom and Northcutt got there, Daniel had wolfed down one plate of beans and was working on a second. Flor gave the two men a good drink out of the *pulque* jug. When Northcutt looked around for another drink, the jug was gone. "I can't afford to keep *you* in whisky," Flor said. "I ain't fixin' to try."

Methodically she cleaned Daniel's wound. "If they'd hit you any harder, the brains'd be oozin out," she told him. "But I'm not sure you got any; if you did you wouldn't of took up with the likes of Milo Seldom. Anybody can tell you he's got two left feet."

Seldom shrugged off the insult. It was of small moment to him in the face of a good meal. "Flor, I reckon you know they got that tobacco."

She nodded.

"There goes our trip after that silver. All the hopes I had was ridin' in them packs. Times it seems like the good Lord has got a grudge against me, and be damned if I can figure where I ever done Him a wrong turn."

"I saw it through my window, before I took out the back and left here. It ain't your tobacco no more, Milo."

Milo said dejectedly, "I'm glad I at least had the use of it awhile and could favor a few good folks like Daniel's daddy with a handful of it. I tried to be generous while I had it. Now I'm hopin' you'll be generous, Flor."

She looked at him quizzically, not answering. He went on, "We been left afoot. No horses, no guns, not a morsel of food to keep us from starvation. I was hopin' you'd find it in your heart, Flor, to help us get a little stake. If not for me, for this good farmer who left home and family to come help us. If we'd of found the silver, we'd of done well by you, Flor. We'd of bought you finery like you've never seen, and a house bigger than the San Fernando church."

"I'll bet," she said dryly.

"It's the Lord's truth. Have I ever lied to you, Flor."

She just stared at him.

"We've come upon evil days, Flor. I know that in

89

spite of tryin' to act like Jezebel, you got the heart of a sweet angel. We're on your mercy."

No mercy showed in her eyes. "If I'll stake you, will you turn over to me all claim you got on that tobacco or the money that comes out of it?"

"You're just a woman, Flor. You got no chance . . ."

"I didn't ask you that; I asked if it's a deal."

Seldom shrugged, having nothing to lose. "Sure, it's a deal."

She glanced at the other men, each in turn. "You all heard that. You're my witnesses." Daniel nodded dully, figuring it was a waste of time. Soon as he was able, he would leave here anyway, striking out for home. He didn't know how he would explain his coming back afoot, no horse, no saddle, no rifle. It would be a humbling thing.

Flor said, "Was I to get the tobacco, I'd need help to go down to the border with me to sell it and to find my no-account father. Would you-all go with me? Would you take orders from me and not argue like a bunch of burro traders?"

Seldom said, "Flor, you're talkin' idle."

"Fine one you are to call somebody else idle. I want an answer—yes or no."

"Sure," Seldom said. "Only, it ain't goin' to happen."

Flor turned to Daniel Provost. "You showed fight against them *ladrones* last night, even if you didn't show sense. And you come in ahead of Milo and Paley awhile ago. I think you might be a good gamble; I'd like you to go."

Daniel looked at her with growing interest; he sensed this wasn't all idle talk. "I don't know that I'd want a woman for a boss."

"Would you rather it was Milo?"

Daniel shook his head. He didn't figure Flor could do any worse.

Flor turned to Paley Northcutt. "No use you sayin' anything, Paley. I don't intend to take anybody that can't leave a jug alone."

Northcutt shook his head in puzzlement. "I don't even know what the hell everybody's talkin' about." Daniel remembered that nobody had ever told him. Daniel said, "He took a right smart of punishment today that was none of his affair. Somebody owes him somethin'."

Flor studied the man in silence. "You know why I can't take you, Paley. How long since you been cold sober?"

"Countin' today?"

"Before that."

Paley rubbed his chin, eyes narrowing in deep thought.

"There was a couple of days back in January. Or maybe it was February. Mexican family run plumb out of wood, and I went to help them gather it against the cold. Dropped my jug and busted it before we got out of sight of town. But I done all right."

"Think you could stay sober for a long time, maybe several weeks?"

Northcutt shrugged. "So far I ain't heard no good reason."

Milo grunted sarcastically. "There *ain't* no good reason. We lost it all."

Floes face glowed in triumph. "Lalo, you want to show them?"

Lalo smiled. "My pleasure. If you will follow me, Milo; you too, my farmer friend." He walked out the door into the moonlight. Milo grumbled about the foolishness of listening to any woman idle away the time, but he followed.

Lalo Talavera pointed toward the brush arbor. "Are those the horses you lost? And the mules?"

Daniel blinked in surprise. There stood his roan horse Sam Houston that the Mexicans had taken from him this morning. There was Seldom's horse, and there were the packmules. He smelled the tobacco even before he saw the packs slung across the rough fence.

Milo Seldom shouted in joy. "The angels will bless you in heaven, Flor. You got it all back for me."

Flor Carmody had come out behind him. Her voice bristled in sarcasm. "For *you?* I'll take my blessin's here on earth. You lost it; it's all mine."

Milo stared in disbelief. "Flor! You wouldn't do that to me!"

She stood like a rock. "The hell I wouldn't."

Milo's voice began to soften, to implore. "Flor, all them things you said in yonder—I took them for idle talk."

"I never idle, Milo; you ought to know that. You heard what I said and you agreed to it. I got enough witnesses to take you to any court in the republic of Texas. But I won't take you to court. Give me any trouble and I'll turn you over to the same friends of mine who took care of Fanch and Bodine."

Milo looked at the tobacco packs. "You didn't have them killed, did you? Ain't no tobacco worth gettin' men killed, even men like them two."

She shook her head. "They're all right, but they're goin' to enjoy the hospitality of some awful stubborn people a few days while I go south with this tobacco."

Milo grumbled. "One thing I don't understand. If you knew where them Mexicans was takin' us, why didn't somebody come fetch us instead of lettin' us walk all the way back?"

Flor said, "I knew you'd get lost soon as they turned you loose. We wouldn't know where to look for you."

"We could've wandered around out there and starved to death."

She shrugged. "Then I'd of had to get somebody else to help me take the tobacco to Mexico."

6

SOUTH OF SAN ANTONIO, DANIEL FOUND THE COUNTRY gradually changing. First it was green rolling hills, then the land took on a drier, harsher aspect hinting at the desert which lay ahead. Vegetation was still plentiful but different in character, much of it cactus-type growth, more of the thorny brush, the catclaw, *gua-jillo,* mesquite. Prickly pear grew in abundance. Along the dim trail Daniel could see evidence of last winter's hard times when Mexican freighters had impaled pear pads on pitchforks and burned the thorns away so they could be fed to the oxen which pulled the lumbering *carretas.*

At one point he saw the charred remnants of several ox-carts. From the looks of them he judged it had been two or three years since they had burned. He could picture shouting Comanche warriors suddenly charging from a nearby motte of heavy brush and overrunning the cart men before they could get into position to stage a defense. Wooden crosses leaned at angles over five graves.

A chill ran up Daniel's spine, and he gave the motte a long study, his hand tight upon the rifle Flor's Mexican friends had recovered for him. He knew it had probably been a while since that brush had hidden a warrior, for raids along these trails were becoming much less common than in an earlier day. But it would be foolhardy to think the Indians were gone forever. Sooner or later they would be back; if it were sooner, Daniel had no intention of being caught asleep.

The thought of Indians made him take another good look at his companions; he had already made several such appraisals and at the end of each was still in doubt. There was, of course, Flor. Her being along gave him cause for worry at the outset; it wasn't seemly for a woman to come on a trip like this. Milo Seldom—well,

Daniel had to admit he was still drawn to this lanky, like-able backwoodsman, but he no longer had faith in Milo's ability to find the back side of a box canyon. Lalo Talavera—he had not yet formed any definite opinion except that for some reason he had not analyzed, the attention the man paid to Flor bothered him; he couldn't say that she encouraged him, but neither did she run him off. Finally, bringing up the rear and leading the pack-mules, were four Mexicans, friends of Flor's. In two days' riding he had learned little about them except that two were brothers, Armando and Bernardo Borrego. The word *borrego* in Spanish meant sheep, and he hoped they didn't act that way if trouble came. The way they followed Flor and jumped at every word she said made him wonder. But then, Flor had a way of making people jump.

Flor had stood by her decision not to take Paley Northcutt. On the face of it, Daniel thought it was a prudent decision, though he regretted the ordeal Northcutt had undergone without even knowing why. Milo Seldom had finally explained to him, after it was too late and Flor had taken over.

"Silver? Solid silver, you say?"

Milo had nodded. "Pure silver cast into shiny bars. Maybe more bars than there are horses in San Antonio de Bexar, just layin' there waitin' for somebody to come and carry them away."

"How come there ain't nobody already done it?"

"Very few men still alive have any real idea where to look." Milo frowned. "Sure wisht you was goin' with us, Paley. Maybe I could talk Flor into another frame of mind."

"I ain't sure I'd even want to go. I try to never make an important decision when I'm sober, and I'm sober now."

Daniel Provost was sober, too—he had never been any other way—and he found himself looking back over his shoulder occasionally, resisting an impulse to turn around and go home.

Twice today he had looked back and thought he glimpsed a man on a horse, far behind them. Both times he had blinked and then stared into the heat waves, but neither time could he find again what he had taken for a man; all he could see was brush. Nerves, he thought. Thinking about Indians always got his hair up a little, and he had thought about Indians a right smart.

He was surprised when Flor Carmody pulled her horse over next to his and rode beside him awhile. She asked, "How's your head?"

"Don't hardly feel it any more, except that it itches a little."

"Healin'. Looks like you'll live." She studied him, and her unabashed curiosity made him uneasy. In a way he wanted to pull away from her, but he didn't. He had the feeling he sometimes got when Lizbeth Wills was near him but not quite touching. She said, "You been worryin' over somethin'. Want to talk about it?"

"Just been thinkin' about Indians some."

"We don't none of us live forever. Anyway, you know there ain't been much Indian trouble on this trail in a long time. You're bothered by more than Indians."

"I'm bothered by you bein' here. This is a man's job, not a woman's."

"Mexican women have always gone with their men; they're not like white women. There were Mexican women with Santa Anna at the Alamo who came all the way up from Toluca to cook for their men and see after their other needs. There've been Mexican women at all the missions and all the outposts. Besides, I've got a lot at stake here; I figure I'm smarter than any man on this trip."

He had no argument with her on that. "Why bring this bunch, then? Why not find you some better men?"

"If they were any smarter, they wouldn't take orders from me. I settle for what I can get."

He glanced back in suspicion at the packmules. "The more I've thought about it, the more I doubt that there's enough money in three packs of tobacco to buy the supplies and mules and such that's goin' to be needed for an expedition out west."

"That was Milo's notion, and he never did have much head for figures. He's a dreamer, not a book-keeper. You're right; three packs won't buy near enough. But I won't be sellin' three packs; I'll sell a dozen or fifteen."

Daniel decided she wasn't much of a bookkeeper either. "I can't see where you'll get them."

"You ever hear them talk much about my father?"

Daniel shook his head. "Not much."

"He's a real blackleg, that old man—a scoundrel if ever one was born. But he taught me aplenty. There'll be a dozen more packs of tobacco when the time comes. Just trust me."

Late in the afternoon Daniel let himself drop back near the packmules, where Lalo Talavera was standing rear guard. He looked over his shoulder and caught a glimpse of what he had taken before to be a horseman. He squinted, but the man—if it had been a man—seemed to melt into the dotting of dark brush.

Talavera said in Spanish, "He is there, then he is not."

"You been seein' him too?"

"Since yesterday."

"Indian, maybe, scoutin' us?"

Lalo shook his head. "Possibly, but Indians would not wait so long to try us out. It is a robber, perhaps, hoping to come at night and find us sleeping. It is probable he tried us last night and saw men on guard."

"Makes me nervous, him trailin' along like that. Keep thinkin' it could be Bodine and Fanch. Next time around, that Bodine's likely to kill somebody."

"When it does not itch, I do not scratch. But since it itches *you,* then perhaps it is best we scratch a little, if you are game for it."

Daniel's mouth went dry. Lalo Talavera was testing him. On reflection, Daniel decided it was high time he tested himself; he might find he did not care to finish this trip. "What'll we do?"

"You ride up and tell Flor that the next time we pass a motte of brush you and I are going to drop out and wait."

"Think I ought to tell her what for? I'd hate to scare her."

"Scare Flor?" Lalo shook his head. "You could not scare that woman if you tied her to the mouth of a cannon and touched fire to the fuse. Believe me, I have tried. She has not given me so much as a chance to touch."

Daniel told Flor what they intended to do. She seemed more angry than alarmed. "Somebody talked too much," she said grimly. "I'll bet I can guess who it was." She cast a hard glance at Milo Seldom, who rode along head down and unaware, his mind a hundred miles away, probably in the midst of that huge cache of silver bars.

Daniel waited until the strung-out group passed by him and Lalo came, bringing up the rear. As they topped a small hill, Lalo pointed to two stands of brush, the faint trace running between them. "When he comes even with us, we shall ride out and take him."

"Alive?"

"If possible, but dead if he shows resistance. We are a long way from sheriffs here, and judges. Where there is no law, one makes it."

Daniel's nervous hands gripped his rifle, and realization came that in a few minutes he would be looking down the sights at a man, possibly to kill him. It was an awesome thought, and he tried to think instead of the farm. It seemed a long way off.

Lalo motioned for Daniel to take the motte on the right, and Lalo rode for the one on the left. Daniel noticed that Lalo was careful to ride where the grass was heaviest, to mask his tracks. Daniel was chagrined that he hadn't thought of it himself.

He hadn't realized how still and close a brushy motte could be, for the heavy foliage cut off any breeze; it cut off any visibility as well, which heightened the feeling of imprisonment. Daniel sensed that the man probably had topped the hill by now and should be on his way down, yet he could not risk stepping out to see. He wondered how he could sweat so much, yet his mouth be so damnably dry. He continually had to wipe his hand on his britches to keep it from being slick against his rifle.

Presently he heard slow hoofbeats against the soft ground, far away at first, then closer. Peering through the foliage, he caught a glimpse of color, but that was all. In a minute now the man would be even with him. Foliage was its lightest at the lower levels of the mesquites, and he caught sight of a horse's feet picking up and setting down. Daniel spurred out into the open, rifle at the ready. Lalo spurred from the other side.

"*Manos arriba!*" Lalo shouted.

The man thrust both arms straight up over his head.

"Fellers, don't you-all shoot! Lalo, it's just me, Paley Northcutt. Farmer boy, don't you let your finger get nervous on that trigger."

Daniel lowered the rifle, but Lalo held his steady. "All right, *borracho,* perhaps you will tell why you have followed us so far."

Paley Northcutt trembled in surprise at being caught this way. "Didn't mean no harm, Lalo; you know there ain't a particle of harm in me."

"Maybe there is and maybe there is not. Answer what I asked you."

"I give a lot of thought to what Milo said about that silver. More I studied on it, the more I wanted to go."

"Why?"

"A few bars of that silver would sure buy a lot of whisky."

Lalo glanced at Daniel. "An honest answer."

Daniel demanded, "How come you followed us instead of comin' in like a man?"

"Flor'd of run me off. I figured if I was to wait a couple or three days till we was a long ways from San Antonio, she wouldn't have the heart to turn me down and send me back through Indian country all by myself."

Lalo said, "You don't know our Flor."

The more Daniel thought about it, the angrier he became, remembering the anxiety that had risen in him like fever while he waited in that hot, still motte. "You know, don't you, that you give us quite a turn?"

"Wouldn't of done it for the world. You-all ought to've ignored me."

"Ignore you?" Daniel demanded incredulously.

Paley Northcutt looked down ashamed. "Seems like folks have always found me easy to ignore."

Daniel's anger ebbed, and he found himself touched by remorse. "I didn't go to holler at you, Paley."

"Everybody does."

Lalo said, "Come on, Paley. We shall see if Flor's heart is as soft as ours. I think she will probably kick you."

She would have, had the long riding skirts not made it impractical. Hands on her hips, she gave Paley Northcutt a bilingual threshing that would have moved a reluctant team of Mexican mules through east Texas mud in a run. She turned finally to Lalo and Daniel. "You ought to have shot him. We got no use for a drunk on this trip, and we can't just send him back. Minute he gets to babblin' over a jug, he'll have half of San Antonio trailin' us to get the silver."

Paley's slumped shoulders straightened. "You mean I can stay?"

"I mean I've half a notion to shoot you myself."

"I ain't drunk now, Flor, and I didn't bring nothin' to drink. Search me; search my saddlebags and blanket. Only thing I got liquid is a goatskin of water."

Flor studied him narrow-eyed and angry. "I don't know . . . ."

Milo Seldom put in, "He's a good ol' boy, Flor. He's a right smart of help when he's sober."

"You can't remember that far back," she declared.

Lalo Talavera nodded Flor over a little closer. "True, he does not look like much, and when he finds whisky he is little of a man. But if you had ever seen his body, *hija,* you would have seen many battle scars, and none of them on his back."

Flor paced the ground, stopping to stare at Paley, then pacing and stopping to glance at the other men. "Looks to me like you-all want to keep him. Damn if I can see it your way, but there ain't nobody ever accused Flor Carmody of bein' difficult. All right, he can stay, but I want one thing understood: he ain't to have a chance of findin' anything to drink. If there's a man here got a drop of anything stronger than water hid out, I want it turned in to me right now."

Lalo Talavera dug into his blankets and fetched a jug. The Borrego brothers looked at each other a moment, then gave in and brought out one apiece. Flor looked sharply at the men. "Is that all? You sure?" One of the Borregos then brought out a second jug. Without ceremony Flor took Daniel's rifle from his hand. She pounded the butt of it against all the jugs and broke them. The liquor disappeared quickly into the sand.

Paley Northcutt stared at it as though someone cut the throat of his pet horse.

"We've wasted enough time," Flor said. "Let's get this outfit movin'."

7

IT WAS A BIG, EMPTY LAND WHERE NO ONE LIVED. THE terrain became drier and hotter, the vegetation increasingly scrubby and thorny. Daniel sensed they were approaching the Mexico border even though he had never been there. He knew it by description from men who had fought and bled along that broad, muddy river. He noticed that the nearer they came to the Rio Grande, the more apprehension crept into Milo Seldom's nervous face. Eventually Milo pulled his horse in beside Flor's.

"Flor, I thought you said you knowed this country."

"I do."

"Well, don't you know where this trail is takin' us? There's a thousand miles of river to choose from, and you're stayin' on a trail that takes us right to a Mexican customs house. They'll catch us before our clothes dry out."

"Remember the rule, Milo: I'm in charge of this outfit."

"They got a prison across yonder with stone walls twelve feet high that they built just to put smugglers in. You act like you're tryin' to get the whole bunch of us throwed in there for twenty years."

"Did I ever say I intended to smuggle this stuff into Mexico?"

"Is there any other way? They got a customs duty over there that'd stagger a Tennessee plow mule. Time we pay it, we won't have enough left to buy a sack of cornmeal."

"We won't pay it."

"The only way to keep from payin' it is to smuggle past customs. The way we're goin', we'd just as well be carryin' a red flag and a Mexican brass band."

"You've got lots of imagination, Milo, but it doesn't always run in the right direction. You've known my ol' daddy Cephus a long time. Did you ever know him to do anything straightforward and honest?"

"Can't say as ever I did."

"Well, I'm his daughter. Just be quiet and let me handle this thing."

Milo Seldom pulled away but was far from quiet. He rode up first beside Paley Northcutt, then Daniel, then Lalo and finally the Borregos, telling each in turn that this wild-eyed woman was fixing to get all of them killed or flung into a dungeon to rot. None of them gave him any satisfaction. He came back finally to Daniel. "Farmer, if you're smart, you won't be no party to this. You'll tell her we're taking that tobacco and crossin' the river someplace else."

Daniel had no idea what scheme Flor Carmody carried inside that pretty head, but he had a feeling she was more to be trusted than Milo. "If you'd of been smart," Daniel retorted, "you'd still have the tobacco yourself."

They came to the river at midday. Daniel rode ahead to take his first look at this fabled Rio Bravo whose waters through the years had washed many armies,

105

advancing and retreating, from both the south side and the north—Spanish, Mexican, filibusterers, Texan, not to mention Indian raiding parties which periodically swam south in the full moon and came back with horses and stolen women and children and their lances festooned with fresh scalps from Mexican people who could not conceivably have done them any harm in their own accustomed roaming grounds. This had been a violent river far beyond the memories of living men, back through the times of their fathers and grandfathers. Daniel suspected it might be a violent river for a long time to come.

On the far side, a fair distance up the bank and probably well beyond the flood limits, stood a rambling stone structure with corrals beyond it, flanked on either side by simple *jacales,* small houses of brush and mud. Past that, half a mile or so, stood a town, its mud walls gray, its rock walls catching the sun. This, Daniel thought, would be the place they had been talking about, Colmena Vieja. The word *colmena* meant beehive, *vieja,* old. Probably somebody had kept bees here at some time in the distant past, though on first sight Daniel could not see a thing a bee could make honey of.

He saw activity at the stone building across the river and noted that several men were looking their way. Milo Seldom rode up and said bitterly, "Well, she's went and done it now. That's the customs house, and they've seen us. Ain't no way we can cross that river now without they'll pounce on us like a bobcat on a rabbit."

Flor Carmody heard him but seemed to make a point of ignoring his comment. She said, "Daniel, I'd like you to go across with me to talk to the customs officer." She glanced at Milo. "You can come too if you'll promise to keep your mouth shut no matter what you see or hear."

Milo nodded sarcastically. "Sure, I'd like to go. I'd like to see how you get us out of this mess."

"We're in no mess. Long as the goods stay on this side of the river, we ain't broken no law."

"And we get no money for them."

"Have faith, o brethern, and all things will be revealed unto you."

Grimly Milo said, "Don't be makin' light of the Word."

She turned to Bernardo Borrego and said in Spanish, "You keep a watch on Paley Northcutt and see that he does not cross that river. I do not want him within a mile of any whisky."

Paley said in a hurt voice, "I heard that. You can trust me."

"So long as Bernardo watches you, I can." She dropped everything off her saddle, touched a spur to her horse, trotted him down the bank and plunged off into the river. Her skirts flared out as the water lifted them, and she slid out of the saddle to give the horse an easier go of it. She held onto the reins but left them loose, and she gripped the saddlehorn.

Daniel let his blanket and his warbag to the ground and knotted the powderhorn string up tight so that the horn was close to his neck. He followed Flor into the river, despairing of being able to keep his rifle dry. But he decided it wouldn't make any difference; he wasn't going to shoot anybody over there.

The river was deeper and swifter in the middle than he had expected. He almost lost his hold on the saddlehorn and let himself slip back to wrap his hand in the horse's tail. Daniel did not dare lose his hold; he was not a swimmer. He caught a mouthful of water and nearly strangled.

By the time they reached the other side he was thoroughly tired of the Rio Grande. He waded out, still holding the horse's tail and letting it pull him along. Coughing heavily, he tried to clear the muddy water from his lungs, his legs shaking from the ordeal. The wind went through the wet clothes and made him cold. He turned his gun barrel down and let the water pour out of it. He would have to give it a good cleaning tonight to keep rust from setting in. Abusing a rifle this way went contrary to all his frontier instincts.

He saw Flor trying to brush her soaked clothing, a lost cause. He supposed it was a woman's nature to try to salvage something of her appearance in even the most adverse of circumstances. And these were very adverse.

Three horsemen trotted down from the customs house. The one in front was an officer, Daniel figured, because his uniform had once been brighter and more colorful than the plain dingy white of the others. All were threadbare now and showed the results of hope-less battle against sweat and grime and heavy wear. The officer looked first at Daniel, then at Milo, trying to decide which man was in command here. Flor left him in doubt for only a moment.

"Captain," she asked in Spanish, "are you the customs officer here?"

He smiled then, eyes warming to the slender girl, her wet clothing clinging tightly to her body. "*Sí, señorita,* I am in charge here. But you give me a promotion my superiors have not chosen to do. I am but a lieutenant."

"Surely," said Flor, "you should be a captain, or perhaps even higher. One can tell from here that you keep a tight discipline and an efficient post."

"Again my thanks, *señorita.* If there is any way I may serve you, I am Lieutenant Zamaniega, *a sus ordenes.*"

"And I," said Flor without a sign of guile, "am Flor de Zavala y Campos. My father was Rafael Zavala the merchant. Surely you knew him."

The lieutenant shook his head. "The name unfortunately does not bring the man to mind, but I am sure it was my loss not to have known him. Again, how may I serve you?"

"I have across the river the remnants of a packtrain of goods my father was bringing to Mexico for sale. Alas, he was killed along the way." She crossed herself, and for good reason, Daniel thought. "We were lucky to escape Comanches with our lives, and to bring even this much of the goods."

The lieutenant was squinting, trying to see what lay across the river. "It is a great pity, *señorita*. I shall notify the priest, that he may light a candle."

"I shall see the priest myself, thank you. Meantime, there is the matter of three packs of prime tobacco."

The officer's brown eyes lighted. "Three packs. I fear that will carry a heavy duty, *señorita,* a most heavy duty. I wish there were something I could do for you."

Daniel figured he was giving Flor a chance now to offer him *a mordido,* a bribe to undervalue the goods. He could see larceny in the calculating eyes.

Innocently Flor said, "I feared that would be the case. I hope there will be money enough left to buy mules so that we may go back and get the rest."

"The rest?"

"The other twelve packs of tobacco. We lost most of our mules in the attack. We had to secrete the packs until our return."

The officer looked toward the river, his eyes calculating even faster. "Three packs—twelve packs. That is fifteen packs altogether, a great deal of money."

"Far too much money for a woman like myself, whose business experience is so sadly limited. My father was skilled at the bargaining, but I fear that I know little. I will be gobbled alive like a lamb by the wolf pack. I probably will never be able to retrieve the rest of the goods. I wish I could find an honest and reliable man here to become my partner, to see that I get full value and am not cheated. And that the import

110

levies are fair. He would be rewarded." She looked at him with eyes helpless as a cornered fawn's. "*Well* rewarded, *capitán.*"

Lieutenant Zamaniega bowed from the waist. "*Señorita,* you are most fortunate that you have come to this place rather than some of the thieves' dens that one finds at many points on this river. Our merchants are honest, and generous to a fault. Besides, I shall be vigilant that no man cheats you; on the contrary, I think they will be happy to pay you a premium. I shall personally see to it."

"I had thought that I would test the market here. If it is good, when I retrieve the rest of the packs I shall bring them here also."

"Rest assured, beautiful lady, there is not a better market on the entire Mexican border than you will find right here. We shall see that you are bountifully paid for the goods you have now, and for the rest when you bring them. It is the least we can do for so lovely a woman, so newly bereaved."

Daniel could not trust himself to look at the officer any longer, or at Flor. He looked instead at Milo and found the backwoodsman slumped, mouth slacked open in total disbelief. Daniel beckoned Milo to one side where the officer would not hear. "She always been able to lie like that?"

"She's her daddy's daughter. Ol' Cephus never drew an honest breath."

"I thought he was your friend."

"Cephus Carmody is nobody's friend. I always liked

111

him, but I never turned my back on him when I had anything I thought he'd steal."

The officer told Flor he would be glad to cross the river and give her a customs valuation on the tobacco so she would know exactly what the duty would be before she left the Texas side. "We have a boat tied just upriver," he said. "It will not be necessary for you to swim and cause yourself further discomfort. Would you care to accompany me?"

"I would be delighted, *capitán*. What of my two employees, these *Americanos* here?"

"Do you always give employment to *Americanos?*" The lieutenant plainly disapproved.

"My father's doing. But I must say they fought well against the Comanches—for *Americanos,* at least."

The lieutenant frowned at them. "Alas, the boat is small. If you wish them to be there, I fear they must swim."

A little of the devil was in Flor's eyes as she turned to Milo and Daniel. "You may stay here if you wish, or you may go back the same way you came."

Milo watched sourly as Flor and the officer went to the boat. "This is too much, the way she's kickin' us around like a couple of hound dogs. I swear, I don't know why I stand for it."

"For the same reason I do—all that silver."

"I reckon. Well, friend Daniel, me and you got us an interest across the river. We better get goin'."

"I'd rather stay here." The thought of that muddy water gave him a queasy feeling.

"Stay if you want to. I'm seein' after my interests." Milo plunged off into the river. Daniel hesitated, then did likewise. He found it less of an ordeal the second time, now that he knew what to expect and how to meet it. He and Milo waded out somewhat ahead of the officer's boat and were waiting when Flor and Zamaniega came trudging up the sandy bank. Lalo and the Borregos had seen the customs officer coming and had unloaded the packs from the mules, spreading them out for inspection.

Flor worriedly told the lieutenant, "I fear we have no money with us; that was lost in the battle. Whatever the duty, we must pay it from proceeds or in kind."

The officer opened one of the packs at random and ran his hand down into the burley. He rolled the bright leaves between his fingers, bringing them up to his nose. "Ah," he sighed, "this is rare quality." He smelled the tobacco for a moment, then brought up a small leather bag. "May I?" Flor nodded, and the officer stuffed the bag with the leaves. Done, he put away his smile and momentarily took on the stiff attitude of an official doing his duty.

"*Señorita,* when I send my written accounts at the end of this month, I shall report to my superiors that I found you had three packs of very inferior goathides. Therefore I levy a duty of twenty pesos, payable upon sale of this poor merchandise. Agreed?"

"You are most generous, *mi capitán.*"

"The least one can do for a lady in mourning, and so charming a partner. And now to the boat with these

113

packs. I think I know some merchants who will beat a pathway to your door to bid you a handsome price for these *goathides*." He paused. "And your door will be my door. I offer you the hospitality of my own poor house."

Flor arched her eyebrows. "*Capitán . . .*"

The lieutenant hurried to alter his approach. "But only under the most proper conditions, of course. You shall have total privacy."

"I shall consider it, *mi capitán.* But first, to business, *sí?*"

They loaded the boat. Flor walked away from the lieutenant briefly to give orders to her own men. "Paley, I want you to stay here and watch our belongings. Bernardo, I want you to stay and watch Paley. If he even looks toward that river, shoot him. The rest of you follow us across and bring the mules."

Milo protested, "Flor, I don't know why in the Lord's sweet name you want to lie so shameful. The only honorable thing for us to've done would've been to smuggle that stuff across in the first place. And anyway, where's Cephus Carmody at?"

Flor looked at Lalo Talavera. "Lalo, if Milo does not keep quiet, take him to the river and drown him."

Milo grumbled as he watched the lieutenant help Flor into the boat, holding her hand longer than necessary, then stepping into the boat and seating himself close beside her. He groused, "He's workin' almighty fast."

Lalo observed, "And so is she. Trust her, Milo. She has eyes like a hawk, and talons too."

"I know all about them talons. She's dug them into me."

The river no longer held any dread for Daniel, and he led the way into it, following in the gentle wake of the rowboat. Urged on by the other men, the mules plunged in after Daniel and swam across. Before long the tobacco was on the mule's backs again, dry and in good condition. The lieutenant said he would lead the way to his house, where interested buyers could come and make their bids. "I myself shall go among them this afternoon and tell them what we—*you* have for sale."

"I hope," Flor said worriedly, "I can get enough for this tobacco that I may buy extra mules and supplies and go back for the rest."

"I believe you will be pleasantly surprised, fair lady. I think I may even find a dealer in mules who will be willing to offer you everything you need at a price better than you would expect."

Flor blinked back the tears. "*Mi capitán,* you are a comfort to me in this time of trial."

As they moved up toward the customs house, Daniel noticed a group of men trudging along afoot, accompanied by rifle-carrying horsemen. They were obviously prisoners. He heard Flor ask the lieutenant about them. The officer said, "They are from the prison. They go out to work upon the irrigation ditches belonging to the warden's brother. He considers it a mercy to the men to be allowed to get out into the fresh air and do invigorating exercise. And if thereby they can improve the fields of his brother, then everyone has been the richer for it."

Especially the warden's brother, thought Daniel.

The men were a dirty, bearded lot, many wearing clothes reduced to little better than rags. As they passed, a few shouted vivid suggestions at Flor. One of the men had a gray-laced beard eight or ten inches in length, and his long, tangled hair resembled a bush. He stopped and stared at Flor until a guard took his foot out of the stirrup and gave the man's shoulder a hard push. "Go along, old goat; she is much too young for you."

"Obviously criminals," Flor said to the lieutenant.

"To a man. The world would be better if they could all simply be shot, as *el presidente* wisely did to the *Americanos*." He glanced back at Daniel and Milo, making it plain he had intended them to hear.

In a way Daniel was glad he had heard. Earlier he had worried that Flor was about to pull some kind of swindle and knew his conscience was likely to trouble him. Now he knew his conscience would be no problem.

The customs officer led the way to his house, which to Daniel's surprise was among the larger ones in the town. Daniel wondered how he was able to afford it on the meager salary a customs officer would draw in a town of such modest size. He assumed there was additional income, though he did not speculate upon

116

the nature of it. "The packs may be unloaded here upon the veranda where the merchants may come and examine the merchandise," he told the men. "And you, dear lady, are welcome to come into the house. But first let me go and make sure that the proper preparations are made. Will you excuse me?"

The lieutenant handed his reins to Milo, who resentfully passed them to Daniel. Daniel dropped them. If the horse wanted to wander around town, let him. Daniel looked over the front of the building and then rode to the side to see the rest of it. He saw a handsome *señorita,* obviously agitated, beating a hasty retreat out the back door. He's preparing the way for Flor all right, Daniel mused.

The lieutenant came out in a few moments, followed by an elderly dark-skinned woman, evidently a housekeeper. "My house is your house, *señorita.* The *dueña* will help you find some suitable clothes. I have a trunkful which belonged to my mother, bless her memory."

Daniel figured it was the lieutenant's "mother" he had seen going out the back door.

"You are kind," Flor smiled. "And what of my men?"

"There is a stable in the back. They may make themselves comfortable in the hay if they do not find more desirable accommodations about the town. I believe if they care to look, they can find that Colmena Vieja offers better attractions. And now I go to alert the merchants and a mule dealer. They should begin to arrive within an hour or so. I shall be on hand to see that you are not cheated."

Flor and the men watched the lieutenant ride up the dusty street past playing children and scratching chickens and barking dogs. The feigned helplessness left her face, and her mouth went hard. "He has plans for me. He'll talk the merchants into givin' me a big price to be sure I come back with the rest of the pack-train. Then they'll rob me blind."

Milo said tightly, "That ain't the only plan he's got for you."

She went into the house where the *dueña* waited. Daniel was sure she was gone an hour, possibly more. He had observed with Lizbeth that when a man waited upon a woman, time went by on its knees. She came out finally, in a shiny green dress of some fine material the likes of which Daniel had never seen. She smelled of perfume, her face scrubbed and evidently creamed with something only the women knew of, her black hair freshly combed and pulled back tightly into a bun. A flat-crowned hat sat atop her head. Daniel stared, holding his breath. She was prettier than he had imagined she could be. She bore little resemblance to the Flor Carmody he had seen scrubbing clothes on the bank of the San Antonio River, or had watched coming up muddy and wet from the waters of the Rio Grande.

Flor said, "The lieutenant's mother had good taste."

Daniel said, "I seen his mother. She's younger than *he* is. What's that pretty material?"

118

"Silk. Ain't you ever seen silk before?"

"I reckon not."

She shook her head. "I've seen it, but I ain't never wore any."

"It looks real fine on you."

Flor Carmody gazed at him a moment in surprise. "Farmer, I'm beginnin' to be glad I brought you along."

Daniel was flustered. "I just said what's true."

"But nobody else has said it. Not Milo Seldom, not even that gift to womankind, Lalo Talavera. Somebody brought you up right."

"I've got a good mother."

The other men stared at her, and Daniel decided he didn't like what he read in their eyes. Even Milo Seldom seemed unprepared. "I never seen you thisaway, Flor."

"If we find what we're goin' after, this is what I'll be wearin' from now on, only I won't be anyplace *you* can see me. I'll go to New Orleans or Mexico City or someplace. I'll let them high-nosed *ricos* in San Antonio take just one look at me so I can tell them to go to hell; they'll sit up and take notice."

Milo turned sour again. "They sure will. They'll figure you for one of them high-priced ones."

She flared. "What do you mean by that?"

"I mean there's somethin' undecent about them clothes. Make you look like somebody or somethin' you ain't. You know the kind of women that wears them kind of things. I like you better the way you was, just ordinary."

119

"You think I'm ordinary, do you, Milo?" Her voice was strained; Daniel sensed danger in it even if Milo didn't.

"You sure ain't no silk lady."

She made an angry run at him, and he turned quickly away, trying to get out of reach. She lifted the green skirts and kicked at him. Daniel saw that beneath the silks she still wore her Mexican riding boots.

Milo motioned frantically. "I see people comin', Flor. Probably the merchants we been waitin' for. You better try to *act* like a silk lady."

Flor gained control of herself, though her eyes threatened all manner of violence. She brushed at the dress to straighten its folds and ran her fingers against her dark hair, trying to be sure it was in place. The middle-aged, heavy-set *dueña* watched from the door, confused and suspicious. Daniel wondered what she might later tell the lieutenant.

Testily Daniel said, "Milo, you ought to be ashamed, hurtin' her feelin's that way. She's a lady."

"Her, a lady?"

"She's a lady to me, and you'll treat her like one."

Milo frowned as if something had just come to his notice. "Friend Daniel, I'll have to take to watchin' you a little closer."

Flor was a picture of propriety as the merchants arrived, led by Lieutenant Zamaniega, smiling and protective of the helpless girl. He halted just short of the veranda, surprised by the unexpected beauty of Flor in these fine clothes. He had trouble finding his voice. "Gentlemen, this beautiful lady is *Señorita* de Zavala y Campos. *Señorita,* I would like you to meet these honorable men of Colmena Vieja, *Señores* Vidal, Rodriguez and Sandoval. This other gentleman is *Señor* Ramirez, who may not be quite so honorable because he is a dealer in horses and mules. Nevertheless, I shall be here to see that he treats you fairly." He winked at Ramirez. The men all smiled, Ramirez perhaps the most. They bowed, each in turn.

Daniel could tell they were trying to suppress their eagerness as they inspected the merchandise. They spoke among themselves, hardly above a whisper at first but gradually louder as anger arose with the competition. Zamaniega had stood to one side, quietly admiring Flor. Now he stepped among the three, lecturing them sternly. At last he turned.

"*Señorita,* all three of these gentlemen would naturally like to buy the entire lot, though *Señor* Sandoval has come up with the highest bid. I have proposed that if his price is suitable to you, each shall pay it for one lot of the tobacco; then each will have time to consider what he may bid for the rest of the goods when you bring them."

Flor plainly did not care whether one man got it or all three. "How much?"

Zamaniega beckoned her over to one side. "Let us confer."

Daniel watched suspiciously but could not hear what he was saying. Zamaniega took one of Flor's hands and patted it protectively. Daniel could hear her saying something about the mules. Zamaniega beckoned the mule dealer over and they talked awhile. Ramirez was soon shaking his head angrily, and the lieutenant was lecturing him as he had lectured the three merchants. Ramirez finally shrugged and gave in. Again, smiling in victory, the lieutenant patted Flor's hand. "I told you the merchants of Colmena Vieja are honorable men."

"But how reluctant in their honor," she said.

When the merchants trooped off up the street, the lieutenant began trying to get Flor to go into the house with him, pointing out that the *dueña* was there to see that all was proper. Flor smilingly put him off, telling him there was much that needed to be done in the matter of selecting the mules and the equipment the dealer had promised to furnish, and in buying the supplies needed for the return.

"But," the lieutenant argued, "there should be no necessity to hurry. The good Lord gave few of us money, but He gave all of us the same amount of time. This gift should be used to pleasure the soul as well as to enrich the purse."

"The soul does poorly when the purse is empty. There will be time later when the task is done. If we delay, someone may find our cache and take it."

"Then," he said, bowing, "I leave you and your men to finish the details of the bargain while I return to the routine detail of the bureaucrat. Until tonight."

"Until tonight, *mi capitán.*"

8

FLOR WAS PLEASED BY THE PRICES SHE HAD EXTRACTED, both in selling the tobacco and in buying supplies. "But they're poor liars. You can see in their eyes that they're givin' us the bait the way you'd do to catch a fish. They figure we'll be back and then they'll really jab the hook into us."

They all went together to the various merchants, delivering each his pack of tobacco, then selecting the goods they needed, taking out in cash what they didn't need in trade. Flor spread the business between all three. "If we was to buy everything from one man," she explained to Daniel, "he'd see we're takin' more goods than we'd need for a little trip like we told them about. Time they get to comparin' with each other, we'll be gone."

The way it was, the merchants were glad to trade goods rather than pay all in cash. Daniel noted a considerable discrepancy in the prices each asked for various types of goods. Daniel suspected they had a considerable profit margin hidden away. He noticed that though the general populace of the town was desperately poor, the merchants did not share their plight. Whatever little money found its way into the hands of the people evidently passed on to the profiteering merchants.

At haggling, Lalo Talavera came into most useful service; he was easy with the words, hard at a bargain.

Milo observed, "A merchant is no match for a man as good as Lalo at coaxin' shy women."

The supplies bought and set aside, they went to the mule dealer's before dusk. His corrals were at the edge of town, near sprawling rock walls twelve feet high, guard towers on both sides. There was no gate on the side facing the dealer's, but there was a row of five or six barred windows. "The prison," Milo said unnecessarily; Daniel had already figured that out.

He shuddered. "Bleak-lookin' place from out here."

"Ain't none the better inside," Milo responded. "This is far and away the best view."

Daniel looked up at the guard towers, which stood perhaps six extra feet above the top of the wall. The nearest guard stared curiously at the little group of people approaching the dealer's gate. Daniel knew he looked mostly at Flor. She still wore the silks, though she rode a horse. The long skirts slipped up to show off her riding boots, which was more than most men got to see of a woman other than their wives.

The mule dealer waited, his corrals sporting a selection of animals ranging from fair to indifferent in quality. Right away Flor showed she was not so helpless as her act might have led the dealer to believe. "I have seen the *zopilotes,* the buzzards, turn away in disgust from better than these. If this is the best you have to offer, I must tell Lieutenant Zamaniega we have decided to go to another town."

The dealer quickly protested that she should not act in haste until she had seen his entire offering, that in reality these were but the culls taken out to make selection easier for her; the good mules were in a lower pen and were the ones he had intended to show her from the beginning.

"Milo," she said, "the good Lord left you with many shortcomings, but he did give you an eye for mules. And you, Daniel—as a farmer you're probably good at pickin' animals to work. I'd be obliged if you-all would select them."

It didn't take long. Daniel marveled at the easy skill the dealer's peons showed with the rawhide *reata,* roping the mules as Milo and Daniel pointed them out. The mules came without hesitation when they felt the loop; Daniel suspected they had been taught to expect the other end of the rope if they did not respond.

The deal called for packsaddles and ropes and canvas. Haggling over prices of these was again Lalo's chore; the price of the mules had been set at the lieutenant's house. By a little before dark the deal was made and the mules were led out. Lalo had exacted three extra horses, explaining that they might be needed should the party again encounter Indians.

Clear of the dealer's, Flor told Milo, "I want the supplies boated across the river tonight. We'll take no chance on losin' any of this."

Milo nodded. "You done right good on the tradin', Flor; I'll give you due credit for that. But seems to me like you've forgot one important detail. Without your ol' daddy, this whole thing is nothin' but a pleasure trip, and I ain't seen hide nor hair of him."

"Wrong. You saw him right after we came across the river."

Milo blinked.

"What're you talkin' about?"

"You looked straight at him and didn't know him. His hair and his beard were too long."

Milo's mouth dropped open. "Them prisoners!"

Flor turned in her saddle and pointed her chin toward those gray prison walls. "He's in yonder."

Milo swallowed and looked at the walls and swallowed again. "When did you find that out?"

"Six months ago. It's been nice for a change always to know where he's at."

Milo's face darkened. "How come you waited so long to tell us? We had a right to know."

"When the time came. The time has just now come."

Milo looked for a moment as if he were tempted to hit her. "If Cephus is in yonder, the whole trip is wasted."

"No, it isn't. All we got to do is get him out."

Milo was so angry that he dismounted so he could pace and kick sand. "Bust him out of that prison? You're as crazy as *he* is, and that's some."

"I got a plan. It came to me quick as I saw them marchin' him and them others down the road to the irrigation ditch. Come mornin' we'll just ride down to that ditch and take him away from the guards."

Milo sputtered. "You think it'll be like takin' milk from it baby's lips? In broad daylight, with a long run before we make the river, and with them shootin' at us every step we make, every stroke we swim? And

126

maybe comin' after us, too? There ain't no Texan army on the other side to keep them from comin' across."

"You knew there was risk in this trip before you started."

"Risk is one thing. Suicide is somethin' altogether else."

"You think of a better way?"

"I'll study on it some."

"While you're studyin', the rest of us will be out there by daylight to bust that old man out of jail."

"More likely you'll join him inside of it. Believe me, it's no fit place for man or mule."

Lalo Talavera broke a frowning silence. "For once, pretty lady, I think Milo is right and you are wrong. You should not always keep coming up with surprises."

She held her patience. "That's a habit from handlin' men like you most of my life. The only way is to keep them off balance."

"You have *us* off balance; of that you can be certain."

She turned to Daniel, asking him with her eyes. He said reluctantly, "Milo could be right. Takin' them guards could get somebody killed."

"If it wasn't for the silver, I'd let him stay in there till he rots. But I ain't goin' back to San Antonio empty-handed; I've made up my mind to that. When I go back, people are goin' to lift their heads and take notice. Like it or not, we got to get him out."

They went by each merchant's in turn and packed

the mules. That done, they headed toward the river to hire a boat which would carry the packs across and cut down the risk of soaking the supplies unnecessarily. Daniel figured they would likely soak them in other crossings of other rivers, but there would be time enough later to worry about that. He had about all the worrying he needed right now thinking about breaking Carmody out of prison.

Flor did not accompany them all the way to the river. She chose to stay at the lieutenant's house. "I want to sleep on a real bed instead of a rawhide cot or a wool blanket."

Milo said resentfully, "The lieutenant will be glad to share with you."

"Nothin's goin' to happen. The *dueña* is there."

"Probably too deaf to hear thunder and sleeps like a drunkard."

"I don't see that it's any of your concern."

It was none of Daniel's concern either, but he sided with Milo. "That Zamaniega ain't a man to be trusted."

"No man is to be trusted," Flor said, "so I never have."

She went into the house and out of sight. Daniel watched until he was satisfied she wouldn't show herself again. "Quick as we get that stuff across, I'm comin' back. I ain't just about to leave her here alone."

Milo was only half listening. A notion had come to him; he was vastly pleased with himself. "Don't worry, friend Daniel. It'll be a shorter night than she figures."

They put several packs of supplies in the boat and watched it pull away for its first trip across. Milo still smiled crookedly, keeping his idea to himself.

Daniel began to feel irritated. "You look about to bust."

Milo turned, smiling, "Boys, I got it all worked out if you'll go with me."

Daniel was dubious, for most of Milo's schemes had gone to hell in a handbasket. But he didn't like Flor's, either. "I'll listen to it; that's all I'll promise." Armando Borrego had gone across with the boat, as had a couple of the other men. Lalo had stayed with Milo and Daniel and the mules. Lalo shrugged. "Like the farmer, I will listen."

Milo said, "I can show you easier than I can tell you. When we get the last of the goods across, we'll keep the mules here; we'll need them. We'll need all the men we got, too, except maybe Paley Northcutt. He can stay over yonder and guard the stuff."

It was dark when the last of the supplies had been boated safely to the Texas side of the river and Armando Borrego brought his brother and their two friends with him. Bernardo argued, "The *señorita* wanted me to watch after the Paley Northcutt."

"Paley Northcutt is old enough to watch out for himself," Milo said. "Right now we got need of you on this side."

He led them up the dark streets toward the prison.

Daniel looked about nervously, watching the Mexican people moving like shadows, showing briefly against candlelight and then disappearing in darkness. "Whatever we're goin' to do, Milo, reckon hadn't we ought to wait till everybody has gone to bed?"

"I want us to be done *before* anybody goes to bed," Milo responded. "Especially Flor." He hauled up as the high walls loomed ahead, dark and forbidding. "Besides, we'll attract less attention now than later. There's still lots of people on the streets; us few extra won't be paid no notice of. And when it's over, we'll just get lost amongst the people millin' around."

Daniel looked at the mules and the packsaddles and the ropes. The only thing he could figure was that Milo intended them to throw these ropes over the walls and somehow climb up on them. If that was his intention, Daniel was determined that Milo could go by himself.

Lalo voiced his own doubt. "The wall is there and we are here, and I do not think I like either."

Short of patience, Milo said, "Every prophet in the Good Book was beset by doubters."

"You been a damn poor prophet," Daniel pointed out.

Milo shrugged off the criticism and pointed. "See the barred window? That's where the cells are at. There's four big cells, all on this one wall. Other side's given over to guard barracks and cookin' area and armory and such. The prisoners are kept in these four cells right here."

Daniel demanded, "How do you know?"

"Friend, I been a guest in there."

"How do we know which one Cephus Carmody is in?"

"We don't. We'll just have to bust all four."

Daniel stared, not believing what he had heard. "Just us seven?"

"That's one man for each window and three left over. You couldn't ask for no better odds."

"The hell I couldn't." Daniel's anger began to rise when he thought how Milo had brought them to the foot of these prison walls on a fool's errand. "Milo Seldom, you've had some crazy ideas, that's fair certain. But I swear this is the worst one of all. Bad as Flor's idea was, it beats this. I'm goin' back to watch out for Flor. You comin', Lalo?"

Milo reached out and grabbed his arm. "You-all ain't heard me out. I tell you, it's easy as pourin' water out of a boot. The mules'll do all the work, and there ain't nobody takin' a chance, hardly."

Daniel glanced at Lalo and the others. They seemed inclined to listen, so he decided he would too.

Milo said, "Four windows, three mules apiece. One man will handle each set of mules. I'll take the ropes and go stroll along right by the wall. It's so dark the guards ain't apt to pay me no special attention. They're mostly watchin' the yard anyway; they sure ain't lookin' for anybody tryin' to bust in from outside. I'll pass one end of the rope up to somebody through each window and get them to tie it to the bars."

Daniel considered the plan, skeptical at first. But the more he thought on it, the better chance it seemed to have, even if it did come from Milo. *Everybody* had to win once in a while.

They were stout ropes, and there were plenty of them, so Milo took three coiled ropes per window, one per mule. He put the coils over his arms and walked slowly, falling in behind a strolling Mexican family until he had made his way across the street to the wall. He stopped there, testing to see if the guards in the towers showed any response. Daniel watched closely, holding his breath. He saw no sign that Milo had been noticed.

Milo gave the guards plenty of time, then began walking slowly again, right against the wall, until he came up beneath the first barred window. The bottom of it was a couple of feet above his head. Listening intently, Daniel could not hear him call to the men inside, but he assumed Milo must have done so. He saw a hand reach down to meet Milo's hand, and saw the ends of three ropes go up. Milo paused, again waiting for guard reaction. Seeing none, he dropped the three ropes and moved on.

It took him only a few minutes to make the four windows, though Daniel would have sworn at the time that it took an hour. He could not see any movement at the third and fourth windows because of the distance and the darkness, but he could tell from Milo's actions that all was going well. When Milo dropped the last set of ropes, that was a signal for Armando

Borrego to start in with his three mules. In a moment Bernardo followed, and then Lalo and finally Daniel. Daniel felt his heart thumping, and he resisted a strong inclination to hurry. That, he knew, would stir the suspicion of the guards, for nobody tried to hurry a set of mules.

Daniel reached the ropes beneath his window and halted the mules. As casually as he could, he picked up the ropes one at a time, making sure they were not entangled, and tied each securely to a mule. He thought surely he would be seen, or one of the others would be seen, but it was as Milo had said: nobody ever tried to break into prison, only *out*.

At the window he could see prisoners clamoring to look, excitedly encouraging him to strike those mules smartly and break open this accursed stone wall. He tried to hush them, but they couldn't hear him for the noise they were making. He wondered how the guards could miss it.

"*Andele, hombre!*" somebody shouted from inside the cell.

A guard on the center tower came awake. "*Quien vive?*" he called suspiciously. He could as easily have been looking at one of the other three, but somehow Daniel knew *he* was the one under surveillance.

He heard Milo's shout at the far end of the wall and broke into a trot, leading the three mules. Then he stepped aside and shouted "Hyahh!" slapping the nearest one on the rump with his hat. Before they hit the ends of the ropes, they were running.

133

The ropes jerked taut with a whispering sound, and Daniel heard the crunch of the iron bars being wrenched loose from the stone that held them. The mules stopped abruptly, one going down threshing. Quickly Daniel got in front of them, helped the down mule to its feet and began tugging at them, urging them, to pull hard against the bars.

He was too busy with his own problem to do more than glance at the others in the party. He saw that Lalo's mules had broken their bars completely out of the wall at the first try, and shouting, cheering prisoners were crowding out through the hole like so many happy ants. Daniel kept urging his mules, and the prisoners in the cell pushed against the bars. Suddenly they jerked free and the mules knocked Daniel to the ground as momentum sent them surging forward. He got a hoofmark on his left ribs in the excitement, losing half his breath. But this was no time to be lying in the street. The guards were shooting indiscriminately into the darkness, among the fleeing prisoners. Fortunately they were slowed by the effort of reloading their rifles after every shot.

Milo was running up and down the wall shouting, "Cephus! Cephus Carmody!"

Prisoners came swarming out of the ruined wall through four gaping holes, clambering, scrambling down amidst the fallen stones. No one responded to Milo's call. "Cephus! Cephus Carmody, we come for you!"

One of the guards seemed to have found Milo

Seldom and to have concluded that he was the source of the trouble. He fired, and Milo stumbled. For a breath-stopping moment Daniel thought he was hit, but Milo got up and began running again. He lost all sign of religion.

"Cephus! Goddamn your soul, Cephus Carmody, we're bein' shot at out here! Where the hell you at?"

Daniel was almost run over again, this time by fleeing prisoners. One grabbed and hugged him in the Mexican *abrazo* of friendship, which Daniel thought was not the brightest idea in this time of danger. He caught his mules but almost lost them again in the excitement.

In a minute the cells were empty. All the prisoners had disappeared into the night, leaving only a lingering of dust. Milo Seldom ran once more along the wall, shouting for Cephus Carmody and getting no answer.

Well, almost none. From the top of the wall now came a steadily increasing fire as extra guards came on the run, shooting at anything they saw move. They saw Milo Seldom move very rapidly, running for the other side of the street as hard as he could go. Bullets kicked up dust around him, but in the darkness the guards could not see their own sights. Milo plowed past Daniel, unable to speak but only waving his hand for Daniel to come a-running.

Guards and officers began streaming out, shouting in anger, shooting at anything which moved or seemed likely ever to move.

Somehow the seven men from San Antonio got together where they had left their horses, and all had their mules but Bernardo. Two of his had been taken from him by fleeing prisoners, and the other had been brought down by a guard's bullet. Daniel could see they had no time to talk it out or to worry over Cephus Carmody now; pursuit was on their heels.

"Armando, you and Bernardo take these mules and get across the river, and take your two friends with you," Milo said. "Me and Daniel and Lalo, we'll show ourselves and try to lure the police off of you."

Nobody took time to discuss or argue. The four Mexicans led the mules away. The other three men swung onto their horses, Milo taking the lead.

As first pursuit came around a cluster of stone houses, Milo shouted, "Thisaway, boys," and loped out, away from the direction the four had taken with the mules. Daniel and Lalo followed him as fast as their horses would run. Bullets smacked into walls beside and beyond them. Daniel didn't catch a breath until they had clattered across the flagstone floor of a big patio and through an open iron gate that put them momentarily out of direct line of fire. Shouting and shooting, mounted guards came galloping after them. Milo led them a twisting, turning chase, up one alley, back down a side street, through another patio, out into the open chaparral, then back into town.

At last he reined up, Daniel and Lalo close beside him. They could hear men shouting out in the brush.

"Lost them, at least for a little bit," Milo said tightly.

136

"While we can, we better get Flor and swim the hell across that river."

They loped up to the front of the candlelit house. Milo jumped to the ground and hit the door in a run. Through the open windows Daniel saw Flor still in green silk, seated at a table and sipping wine with Zamaniega. Milo grabbed her around the waist so abruptly that she dropped the wineglass; it shattered on the tile. Zamaniega jumped to his feet in protest, turning his chair over with a clatter. Milo gave him a push that sent him stumbling back to fall ingloriously on his rump, cursing in a manner unbecoming an officer and a gentleman.

Flor's language was little better. As Milo carried her outside, she beat at him with her small fists, demanding that he put her down. Daniel brought her horse around. Milo gave her a boost up. "Grab ahold," he said curtly. "We got a hard ride to make and damn little time to do it in."

By now the alarm had gone up and down the streets, and shouting voices met the angry lieutenant at his front door. Milo heeled his horse into a hard run, straight for the river. Flor kept shouting for some explanation until the first shot was fired from a hundred yards behind them; then she just leaned low over the horse's neck and rode.

Milo said, "We decided if we had to run anyway, we'd rather do it in the dark. So we busted the prison wall down."

"Then, where's the old man?"

137

"He didn't come out."

Flor Carmody cursed like a muleskinner. "Damn you, Milo Seldom, I hope we all live through this. Then I can kill you myself!"

They hit the water in a run. Daniel could hear horses running behind them, but didn't take time to look back. He slid out of the saddle to allow his horse more freedom; he held onto the tail. He heard shots, and bullets plunking into the dark, swirling waters around them.

One of the horses screamed and began to thresh; it was Flor's. She was suddenly cast loose in the water, flailing her arms, going under and coming up gasping. She couldn't swim.

Milo Seldom cried, "Flor!" and quickly left his own horse to try to swim toward her. Then he too was splashing helplessly, for he couldn't swim either. Swimming was a talent few frontiersmen developed.

Daniel knew that if he turned loose of his horse he would be helpless too; they would all drown. But he got hold of the reins and managed to pull his horse around so that he was able to grab Flor. Her hands desperately clutched at Daniel. For a moment he thought she would drag him down. Then she wrapped her arms around his body and gave him freedom to hold onto the horse's tail.

Choking, she managed to cry out, "Milo! Somebody help Milo!"

Milo Seldom was going down for the second or third time, his horse swimming free far beyond his reach. Daniel saw no chance to reach him. It appeared to him that Milo would drown; he had sacrificed himself in an effort to help Flor.

But Lalo Talavera came up from behind and grabbed onto Milo and pulled him toward his own horse. Milo's hands closed over the horse's mane, and it was plain that only death would pry them loose.

The shooting continued, a bullet kicking up water here and there, but in the darkness it would be only pure luck if the men on the south bank managed to hit anybody or anything. Daniel was too busy hanging onto Flor and the horse to try to look back, or to worry much about the rifle fire.

They came up finally on the Texas side. Knees shaking and weak, Daniel somehow found strength to carry Flor up the soft, sandy bank. She was still choking, coughing up water. He looked back at Lalo half dragging Milo Seldom. Milo's horse had come out ahead and had been caught by someone in the shadows beyond the bank.

Flor held onto Daniel long after they were out of the water, her body trembling with cold. It was the first time he had had his arms around her, and he didn't really want to put her down. Even with the distraction of the other excitement, he found himself stirred by her.

But this was no time to be thinking of such things. For all he knew, the pursuers might be swimming that river after them. He found one of the packs of merchandise which had been unloaded earlier from the boat, and he set her gently upon it. Her hands lingered on his arms a moment while she whispered, "Thanks." He quickly found a blanket and wrapped it around her shoulders and the ruined silk dress. She still coughed a little as she watched Lalo Talavera struggle toward them, supporting Milo Seldom.

Voice thin, she said, "You saved my life, Daniel."

"Milo tried to."

"Milo!" He thought he could hear her teeth grind. "I wish he'd drowned!"

Lalo let Milo drop at Flor's feet. He lay coughing, spitting up water. Scathingly Flor demanded, "You want to tell me about it now, Milo?"

He was in no condition to talk. Flor lifted her foot as if to kick him, thought better of it and put her foot down. "Well, Milo, you've done it again. I don't see how one man, all by himself, can manage to do so many things wrong."

Daniel said, "He wasn't by himself, Flor. We was all in on it. The idea didn't sound bad at the time."

"Well, it's sure knocked the bottom out from under us now. They'll be watchin' this river like eagles. We'll have to go back someplace and camp and wait till the excitement has died away before we can make another try at gettin' the old man out of there."

Milo finally had his breath back. "I'm sorry, Flor."

She gritted, "You—" and lifted her foot again. "Aw, what's the use? Your mama ought to've drowned you like a kitten the day you was born. You're like some ill-bred colt with two left forefeet that stumbles as

140

long as it lives. Lord help you, and help all them that touch you. Let's get this stuff on the mules and leave this river before they decide to swim over after us."

The final indignity had not yet come. They found Paley Northcutt lying flat on his back, humming foolishly to himself, a jug of *tequila* sitting within easy reach.

Flor turned angrily on Bernardo. "I thought I told you to watch him."

Milo coughed. "I figured we needed Bernardo; I sent for him."

Flor walked off into the darkness to be alone, but her angry voice left a troubled wake.

9

NOW AND THEN SOMEONE CAME UP OUT OF THE RIVER, and Milo would tense, ready to run. But always it was prisoners they had liberated from behind the high walls, swimming over to freedom by ones and twos and threes. None showed any disposition to cause trouble, but Daniel saw to his powder. He knew some must be hardened criminals; they weren't all in prison simply because some official didn't like the cut of their sandals. How these men planned to subsist in this alien land north of the river Daniel did not know; he doubted if many of them knew. Their first concern was to secure their freedom. Bread and beans at the moment were secondary; but subsistence would soon become a primary worry, for there was little here a man could do to feed himself if he had no gun, no knife, nothing but his hands and the rags he had worn in prison.

Flor had the same notion. "It'd be easy for a bunch to jump us in the dark."

Lalo said, "They should be grateful to us; we set them free."

"Gratitude is for when a man's not hungry. We better pack them mules and move off aways from the river till we decide what to do next."

Paley Northcutt was so helplessly drunk they had to tie him to a horse. Where he had gotten the jug, no one had figured out. "A man like Paley, he has his ways," Milo said experimentally, testing to see if Flor's bitterness toward him had abated. It had not.

She snapped, "Milo, if I hear your voice once more tonight, I'm liable to lose control and shoot you."

Milo stepped back and put a horse between himself and Flor.

Having lost her own horse to a bullet, Flor used the saddle and the horse they had intended for her father. They rode north in darkness to a place where Milo knew of a waterhole, reaching it after daylight. They made camp and ate a little. At that point they gained an inkling of the source of Paley's *tequila*. Some of the coffee was gone, evidently traded to a passer-by. By now Flor was too wrung out for anger. She said the coffee wouldn't be much good to them anyway; about all they could do was give up the quest and go back to San Antonio.

142

Daniel spread Flor's blankets in the shade of a mesquite and stood back to watch her stretch out in the ruined silk dress. It was dried and wrinkled now, streaked by water and mud. "Anything I can bring you, Flor?"

"Just keep them the hell away from me till I get some sleep and do some thinkin'."

Milo Seldom came up cautiously, glancing back over his shoulder as if to be sure he had room to run. "Flor, I got to tell you somethin'."

"I don't even want to hear it."

"I'm sorry things didn't work the way I figured. I can't imagine why ol' Cephus didn't come out. I'm wonderin' if somethin' has happened to your ol' daddy."

She shrugged. "I don't give a damn about Cephus. If it hadn't been for the silver, he could've stayed in there the rest of his life and it wouldn't have bothered me none."

"Honor thy father. He *is* your father, you know."

"My mother's mistake. Now go, Milo."

Milo stepped back half a pace. "I heard you hollerin' for somebody to save me out of that water. Showed you didn't mean everything you been sayin', Flor."

"I just didn't want you to drown and rob me of the pleasure of killin' you myself."

Milo looked shamefaced. "I'm right here. Fire away."

"I'm too tired to enjoy it now. I'll do it later."

Daniel watched Milo walk away and decided it was a good time to get an apology off his own chest. He knelt beside Flor. She lay looking at him with no particular expression. She had probably told Milo the truth; she was too tired even to be angry.

He said apologetically, "Seemed like a better idea than it was."

Flor just looked at him. "No need to apologize. It was all my fault."

"How do you figure that?"

"I went on a fool's errand and took fools with me." She raised her arm to examine the ruined green sleeve. "Just look at that dress. I was goin' to have me a dozen just like it. Now even this one ain't fit to wear."

"I'll buy you a better one someday."

"With what? I bet you ain't got a coin on you."

"I *will* have, one of these days."

"Not if you keep runnin' with the likes of Milo Seldom. Anyhow, from what Milo told me, you got a girl of your own to buy dresses for."

Daniel shrugged. "I hadn't thought much about Lizbeth lately. She seems an awful long ways off."

"And I'm near, so you think about *me*. But when I'm far off someday, you'll think of that Lizbeth girl again, or some other."

"Flor."

"Don't apologize. You're a man, and you can't help bein' what Nature made you. Was it different, men wouldn't do nothin' but hunt and fish all the time, and the human race would die out. Mother Nature knew

144

what she was doin', only it seems to me like she gave women the bad end of it all."

Daniel said, "I better go and let you rest."

"I wish you would, but first—" She caught his arm and pulled him down and kissed him. "That," she said, "is for draggin' me out of the water."

Surprised, Daniel touched a hand to his mouth where she had kissed him. "If you ever take a notion to fall in again, let me know. I'll be there."

He left her alone. He needed to lie down and rest too, but the aftermath of the night's excitement still ran too strong for him to think of sleep. He walked around camp checking the mules staked on grass, looking over the packs. He glanced at Paley Northcutt, blissfully sleeping the day away. So far as Paley knew, this was still yesterday; he probably hadn't heard a shot fired last night. Well, Daniel thought, I heard enough for both of us. Sounded like Texas and Mexico was at war again.

Lalo Talavera lay on his blanket, watching Daniel. At length Lalo said, "Lie down, *hombre,* take your rest while you can. One never knows when he may need it."

"If I could walk this nervousness out of me, maybe I could sleep."

He went up to the little spring which furnished the water for a tiny creek that almost died stillborn; the sandy soil thirstily drank it up so that the creek ran hardly more than a hundred yards. That, he gathered from what he had seen and heard, pretty well typified much of the Texas-Mexico border country. He could remember many dry spells back in Hopeful Valley, but none had lasted so long as to bring ruination. Here it appeared to be a constant condition.

The tail of his eye caught movement across the rolling prairie. Two horsemen were approaching the waterhole. Daniel hunched over to lower his profile. The longer he squinted, the more certain he was; both men wore some kind of uniform. He backed away from the spring and into the cover of brush, then sprinted down to where the others were trying to *siesta.*

"Soldiers comin'," he said loudly.

Milo Seldom raised up, blinking sleepily. "Soldiers?"

"Couple of them. The uniforms look Mexican to me."

Milo got to his feet, momentarily confused, slow in waking up. "Just two soldiers? I figured they'd bring a bunch if any came at all."

They roused Lalo and the others; Paley Northcutt was still beyond reach. Milo was saying they had better pack the mules and be gone while the going was good. Flor Carmody went to see for herself and came back. "Runnin' from two soldiers don't hardly seem necessary."

Milo suggested, "They may be scouts for a larger troop."

She said, "So they see us run and send back for the others. Best thing is to stay low and take them by surprise."

146

Daniel said, "We didn't shoot nobody last night. I ain't keen on shootin' some poor soldier that's just doin' his duty."

"Any Mexican soldier over here is trespassin' on foreign soil," she said, blissfully ignoring the fact that in a sense they had all done the same thing yesterday. "Anyway, we'll just take them prisoner till we get farther from the border. They've probably never seen Texas anyhow. The education will do them good."

The Borrego brothers moved the mules farther back into the brush. Daniel and Milo and Lalo Talavera took their rifles and spread out on either side of the trail. Milo told Flor to "Git back out of the way!" She didn't; she brought her heavy old rifle and dropped to her knees beside Daniel.

The two horsemen kept coming. Daniel said, "I can't figure what they're doin' over here. They got no jurisdiction."

Flor said, "They got jurisdiction anywhere there's nobody to stop them. A lot of Mexicans cuss Santa Anna for givin' up Texas all the way down to the Rio Grande. Figure they got it took away from them, and maybe they did."

The two men were so near now that Daniel could hear the squeak of their saddles. He leveled his long-rifle, ready to fire if he had to. The two men were almost abreast of him now, no more than thirty feet away. They reined up, suspicious. Daniel's hands tightened on the rifle, and he held his breath.

He heard a voice say, "Now, don't nobody shoot. We ain't Meskin soldiers."

Flor flung out a profanity and pushed to her feet. She said roughly, "All right, boys, you can put your rifles down."

"That's right, boys," the older rider grinned through his graying beard. "We're harmless."

Flor declared, "I didn't say *that*. I just said for them not to shoot you."

This, Daniel realized, was the same bearded, long-haired old man he had seen among the prisoners yesterday on the road, the one who had stopped to stare at Flor. This, then, was the man the whole misbegotten affair last night had been intended for: Cephus Carmody.

"Daughter," Carmody smiled at Flor, "you are a sight for sore old eyes."

Her voice was not happy. "And you are just a sight. Where the hell was you last night?"

Carmody took his time looking over the rest of the group. "Well, daughter, I'll tell you all about it in due time. Right now me and Notchy sure do need us a drink of water. Or coffee if you got it. Or best of all, whisky if there's any around. You don't know how long it's been since we had us a good drink of whisky."

"It'll be a while longer," Flor told him. "You'll settle for coffee."

Carmody got down from the horse. "Coffee, then. Even coffee ain't often come by in the *juzgado*. I

148

swear, daughter, you are somethin' to see. What's that thing you're wearin'?"

She still had on the green silk. "It *was* a dress, till you didn't show up last night." Her voice sounded cold, but Daniel sensed a relief she tried to cover up. Carmody gave her a tight hug. Flor protested, "After you get your coffee, you'd best go down that creek and take a bath. You smell like an old boar."

"Ain't much facilities for bathin' where we been, or any company to bathe for." He turned. "I wisht you'd say howdy to my friend and partner Notchy O'Dowd."

This time Flor's voice was genuinely cold. "I know him."

O'Dowd was a tall slim man, not unlike the outlaw Bodine. As did Cephus Carmody, he carried a beard from his long imprisonment; his hair came down to his shoulders. But despite the hair, Daniel could see how he got his name. A large piece was missing from one ear, a circular piece probably just the shape of somebody's teeth. A little eye-gouging and ear-chewing were considered fair tactics in a backwoods' barroom set-to. O'Dowd's eyes carried no friendliness as he looked over the men surrounding him. He cut his gaze finally back to Milo. "Seems like I know you. Name's Seldom, ain't it?"

Milo nodded. "I was there the night you lost a part of your ear. Wasn't me that done it, though."

"Friend of yours, as I recall. He ever heal up from the carvin' I gave him?"

149

Milo shrugged. "More or less, only nothin' knitted back in quite the same place as it was. In a crowd, he gets noticed."

Cephus Carmody led his horse into the camp and rummaged around for a cup. Finding it, he poured coffee from a pot sitting on coals, held it a moment under his nose, inhaling and closing his eyes. "The prettiest woman that ever lived never wore perfume as sweet as the smell of good coffee."

Flor gave her father time to drain the cup, then she began to press him. "Where the hell was you last night, and how come you're wearin' soldier clothes? There ain't an army in the world would have you!"

Carmody cleared his throat. "Daughter, when I seen you yesterday on the road, you could've cut off my head with a sword and I'd of never bled a drop. I says to myself, I says, 'Cephus, that little ol' girl of yours has got some scheme in her head or she wouldn't be here.' Naturally I thought you'd have somebody throw a rope over the walls or somethin', so I made it a point for me and Notchy here not to be cooped up in no cell last night. I volunteered us to butcher out some goats for the guards' kitchen, and we took our sweet time gettin' her done. How was I to know you-all was goin' to bust the cells open from outside?"

He poured more coffee. "Damn, I wisht you-all had a little somethin' to lace this with. Coffee is fine, but laced coffee is *real* fine." He savored it. "Well, when all the commotion commenced, me and Notchy was as surprised as anybody. There was a couple guards standin' there worryin' awful over what was goin' on outside, so we took us a chunk of wood apiece and laid them boys away for an early night's rest. Then we put their uniforms on and walked out that front gate amongst the others. They was grabbin' escaped prisoners right and left, but they didn't pay no attention to us because we was in uniform. In the dark, what could they tell? When we got the chance, we took the borry of two good horses, and here we are."

Milo was emboldened by the fact that his plan had worked after all, even if only by accident. "All's well that ends well, it says in the Book."

Cephus Carmody looked around. "Seems to me like you got an awful lot of people here just to get me out of jail. Didn't know I was all that important." He turned to his daughter. "Ought to've figured, though. What troubled me most of all that time I was in prison was the thought of my sweet little ol' girl by herself back in San Antonio, helpless, weepin' her pretty eyes out for her ol' daddy."

Flor's voice hardened. "Oh hell yes, I cried a lot."

Cephus Carmody patted Flor's hand. "Well, girl, you don't have to grieve no longer. I'm back amongst the livin'."

"You don't smell like it. I wisht you'd take a bath."

Carmody shook his head at Notchy O'Dowd. "You hear folks say Mexicans don't care nothin' about clean, but her ol' mother was just like her—always raisn' hell at me about needin' to bathe or put on something' clean. That's all lies about them Mexican

151

women; they're as bad as the rest of them to plague a man. I swear, daughter, I just got out of prison; I don't know what it takes to please you."

Flor jerked her chin at O'Dowd. "It'd have pleased me a right smart if you'd of left *him* in there."

"Why, girl, me and ol' Notchy are partners. What kind of a man would I be to bust out of jail and not take him along?"

"I expect he was the cause of you bein' there in the first place, him and his smugglin' scheme."

"Nothin' wrong with the scheme. We just had us a run of ill fortune, is all. You'll like ol' Notchy if you ever give him a chance. He's as good a friend as ever I had."

"That's damn little recommendation," she said sourly, studying O'Dowd with narrowed eyes. "We'll feed you, O'Dowd, and give you some provisions so you can be on your way."

O'Dowd shrugged. "I got nowheres in particular to go. Figured I'd stick with ol' Cephus awhile."

"No need in that. He's among his friends now."

Milo Seldom put in, "Seems to me like we could sure use an extra man or two where we're goin'."

Cephus Carmody straightened. "Where *are* we goin'?"

Flor's eyes stabbed at Milo. "I'll tell you later."

Cephus insisted, "I won't have you tryin' to run off ol' Notchy thisaway; I tell you, I won't have it. Anybody wants to be a friend of mine has got to be a friend of Notchy's too. Him and me, we been through hell together."

"We got us a plan, Papa. We don't need him."

"If there's any trouble, Notchy can give a good account of himself."

"I can tell that by his ear. Don't be askin' me no questions, Papa. Just tell him to take anything he needs and be on his way."

Cephus Carmody sat puzzling, the cup tilting in his hand until it seemed certain the coffee would spill. His eyes widened in sudden conviction. "You're after Bowie's silver! You want Bowie's silver and you can't have it without me. I knowed there had to be some reason you come to get me; you never loved me all that much."

Flor glanced quickly at O'Dowd. "Hush, Papa. You're just guessin'."

"Guess, hell! I got no secrets from Notchy. Him and me, we've talked about that silver a hundred times. That's how come we made that smugglin' trip in the first place, was to try to get us enough money together to go and hunt for that silver." He looked around the camp, seeming suddenly to realize how much equipment and supplies Flor and her party had. "By grabs, girl, I don't know how you done it, but you done it."

She said, "I didn't do it all by myself."

Milo added dryly, "That's the truth if ever the truth was told."

Cephus Carmody's grin swelled into full flower while Flor's frown grew deeper and darker. He said, "Time we get out into Indian country, we'll be countin' our guns and glad for all we got. If you

153

want me, little girl, you got to take Notchy too."

Flor saw she was beaten. She said, "Damn you, Papa."

Cephus Carmody stretched his legs and sighed. "My, but it's good to be back once again in the bosom of my family, amongst them that loves me."

10

AFTER PUTTING AWAY ENOUGH BEANS TO HAVE OVER-flowed a bucket, Cephus Carmody counted the mules and surveyed the good stock of supplies. "By George, this ain't bad at all. We've done right fine."

Stiffly Flor said, "Not we, Papa, *me.* This is all mine."

Carmody's eyebrows lifted. "Yours? I can't think of no virtuous way one girl could've put all this together. I hope you ain't been doin' things that'd shame an ol' daddy's heart."

"You'd of been proud. It took schemin' and under-handedness, and that's about the only thing you ever gave me."

Cephus had to know the particulars, so she told him. The old man nodded approval. "Blood always tells. Too bad you wasn't born a boy instead of a girl. We could've done big things together."

"We still can. We can go for Bowie's silver."

"Apt to be a hard trip. I've told you how it was with me and Bowie and them others. Ain't no place for a frail little ol' girl."

"I wasn't too frail to get this far."

154

"But this was the easy part. You'd be better off to wait for us in San Antonio. We'd bring you your share just like if you'd gone."

"Sure you would, Papa, the first time it ever come a three-foot snow on the Fourth of July. Forget it. I got the biggest investment here, and I'm goin' to protect it."

"You figure all the leverage is on your side?"

"Without these mules and supplies, there ain't *nobody* goin' after that silver."

"Without the knowledge I got in my head, them mules and supplies ain't worth one smoke puff in hell to you. Looks to me like I got a little leverage myown-self."

They stared hard at each other, neither giving an inch. Daniel watched, figuring that sooner or later one would weaken.

"You ain't goin,' girl," Cephus gritted.

"Like hell I ain't. Last time you told me what to do was when I was about fourteen. I'm goin,' Papa, and you'd just as well get that into your thick old skull."

Carmody finally turned away, but he hadn't surrendered; he had just let it come to a Mexican standoff. He muttered something to the effect that the new generation had no respect for anything.

Flor got in the last word. "I respect money, Papa, same as you do."

They packed the mules and saddled the horses and headed north. If they had known just where the San Saba mission lay from here, they could have cut northwest and made directly for it, but Cephus Carmody needed landmarks. These could be had only by going most of the way back to San Antonio, original starting place of Jim Bowie's expedition.

Milo Seldom fell in beside Cephus as they rode, telling him how good it was to see him again, sympathizing over the stubborn and vindictive ways of his daughter. Milo said, "She didn't inherit your kind nature, Cephus. I swear, sometimes she seems like she bites to see how much blood she can draw."

"Just like her mother was, God rest her," Cephus nodded. "A sweet and gentle woman, but *mean*. You go tell Flor we can't take her."

"*Me* tell her?" Milo frowned. "If I was to say the sun rises in the east, she'd say it comes up out of the west just to *dis*pute me. Sometimes it's hard to remember that she's in love with me."

"Well, she ain't goin'. Somehow or other we got to impress her with that fact."

Notchy O'Dowd's face furrowed. "I could impress it on her, you just give me a little slack and stay out of my way."

Daniel was outraged. "You'll have to whip me first!"

O'Dowd glared at Daniel, and Cephus turned in annoyance to Milo. "May I be shot and skinned if this ain't a fresh-mouthed farmer you brought along, Milo. I swear, I ain't too keen on bringin' strangers amongst us on an errand of this nature."

Daniel said defensively, "I got an investment of sorts in this trip."

156

Milo shrugged at Cephus Carmody. "Daniel's a good boy, Cephus. I wager you'll be glad we brung him, only you got to have patience. He was pulled a little green."

Cephus said impatiently, "Well, Daniel, when I was a lad your age, they always taught us to be respectful and listen to our elders, and not talk in where there wasn't no call."

"You start workin' against Flor, I'd say there was a call."

"We're workin' for her own good, boy. She's got no business out in Indian country. You know what them heathens do to a woman when they catch her? Ain't no pretty sight to see, nor to ponder over. I got nothin' but her best interests in my mind."

Milo said, "Cephus is a man with a big heart."

Daniel doubted that, but he kept his doubts to himself. As they made the long trip north, he watched old Cephus Carmody single out the other members of the party one by one and try to agitate them against his daughter. That Flor was aware of it there could be no doubt; the old man's voice carried like the squeaking wheel of an ungreased Mexican cart.

Paley Northcutt having sobered up enough, they quit tying him to the saddle, and he promptly fell off. The second time it happened, Flor commanded, "If he falls one more time, leave him. He can walk and sober up, or he can stay there; I don't care which."

Daniel felt some sympathy for him, though not as much as the other time when he had been taken out from San Antonio and forced to walk back. This time it was his own fault. Paley fell again, but Daniel helped him remount while Flor was not looking.

Paley wheezed, "I gonnies, Daniel, you right sure you didn't bring no whisky back from Mexico? Don't hardly seem natural for a man not to bring along a little drop of kindness."

"We was too busy to think about it."

Paley nodded regretfully. "Sure would ease the miseries if I just had me a little somethin' to smooth the wrinkles out of my innards. You got no idea how they can cramp up."

"I'm sorry. Maybe if you'd just leave it alone . . ."

Paley winced from the pain. "I was sober the first twenty-five or thirty years of my life. There's worse things in this world than bein' drunk." He wiped his watering eyes and caught sight of Cephus, who now was talking to Milo and Lalo. "Ol' Cephus, I reckon he's mighty worried somethin' bad'll happen to Flor."

"She's a grown woman. She's earned a right to do what she wants to."

Paley frowned. "She ain't spoke a word to me. She's got a right to be mad."

"I reckon she has."

"I made her a promise, and I broke it. But, I gonnies, I won't again."

Daniel shook his head. "I'm sure you won't," he said, though in truth he was not sure at all. He figured Paley Northcutt would stay sober only so long as he could find nothing stronger than coffee to drink.

158

Daniel was not with Paley the next time he fell, but Flor was nearby. She caught the horse and held onto the reins. Without a sign of pity, she demanded, "Get on your feet, Paley!"

Paley struggled onto hands and knees, got up into a hunched position, then sank back to his knees, exhausted. Daniel started to dismount and help him. Flor cast him a quick, angry glance. "You stay right where you're at, Daniel. Let Paley get up for himself."

Paley managed it, somehow. He started unsteadily for his horse, but Flor swung the animal around behind her own horse. "No, Paley, I said you'd walk if you fell again, and I meant it."

"Flor, I can't . . ."

"You can if you have to. And right now you have to." Most of the other men had gathered around. She said to them, "Don't none of you move to help him. If he's a man, let him help himself." She motioned for them all to move away. She held back until they did, then came along at the rear, leading Paley's horse. Paley staggered after her, calling a couple of times, then giving up appealing to her. He kept on walking, though his steps were short and painful. Daniel said to Flor, "Even if he keeps walkin', he can't walk as fast as these horses. He'll drop way behind."

"But he'll get cold sober doin' it. And he'll think hard before he pulls that stunt again on this trip—if he even gets the chance."

"The sun's pretty hot. It could kill him."

"You leave him alone, Daniel; let him suffer it out."

159

"And if he dies?"

"We'll bury him. Now you go on up yonder and leave Paley alone."

Daniel knew he ought to argue a little stronger for Paley, but he also knew she wouldn't pay attention. He wasn't ready yet to defy her altogether. He rode on ahead, as he was told. Old Cephus Carmody sat on his horse, watching, the shirt of his uniform unbuttoned all the way down and lifting with the hot wind. "Kind of got a hard streak about her, ain't she, boy?"

Daniel frowned, not caring to share Cephus' company. "She does what she thinks is right."

"A woman always does, and she's often wrong. But there ain't no reasonin' with an unreasonable woman. That's how it was with her mother. I always went ahead and done what I wanted to. She'd cloud up and thunder, and you'd even see a little lightnin', but by and by she'd pick up and come after me. Man don't ever want to let a woman take over the authority, boy. That's a lesson you better learn now; it'll save you a lifetime of grief."

"Flor's still runnin' this outfit."

"But it ain't her place. A woman's place is *behind* her man."

"Flor ain't got a man."

Cephus eyed him with speculation. "So that's it. I been wonderin' to myself why a nice young farmer like you would be along with my daughter on a dangerous scheme like this one. Now all of a sudden I think I see. You got designs on her, ain't you?"

Daniel was scandalized. "Mister Carmody . . ."

"No offense taken on my part, boy. Even if she *is* my daughter, I know how a man thinks. I done a right smart of that in my life, and I ain't too old to do it again given the proper opportunity. But let me tell you right now that a woman don't put out them favors free of charge; she'll make you pay if she can. Don't ever let her get the advantage."

"I got no such intentions toward your daughter, and she wouldn't think of it either."

"Boy, you got a lot to learn. But a trip like this ain't no place to learn it; we got enough other things to worry about without frettin' over the plottin' and intrigues of a devious woman. When we get close to San Antonio, we got to leave her."

"You'll get no help from me."

"Then we'll take no interference from you, either. You better study on that, farmer."

Notchy O'Dowd had dropped back to hear the last of it, and a hard look from him backed up what Carmody had said.

Paley had fallen so far behind that Daniel finally could no longer see him. He turned his horse and back-trailed to where Flor was bringing up the rear, leading Paley's animal. He said, "I'm goin' to see about him."

"You heard what I told you."

"I don't give a damn what you told me. Give me Paley's horse."

She looked at him oddly, more startled than angry.

"I'll go back with you," she said, and hung onto the horse.

Daniel took that as a bit of a victory for each of them and was willing to let her have her part of it. For his own part, he led out and stayed in the lead all the way back to where Paley was doggedly dragging himself one painful step at a time. Paley halted and swayed, tongue running over dry lips as he rubbed sweat from his face onto his sleeve. "I'd of made it, but I'm glad you come."

Daniel said, "We figured Flor had made her point with you."

"Oh, she did; she most certainly did. I'll never again lift a jug to my lips without I think of all the walkin' I done lately."

She said, "That won't stop you from liftin' it though, will it?"

"No, Flor, I'd lie if I told you otherwise."

She shook her head. "Even smallpox can be cured sometimes, but not a hard-drinkin' man. Paley, can you get on the horse by yourself?"

"I reckon I can." And he did. The heat and the walk had burned much of the alcohol out of him.

She said, "You'll kill yourself drinkin' thataway."

"But I'll die with a smile on my face. Ain't many people can say that with a certainty." His gratitude was plain. "I thank you for comin' back, Flor. You got a heart of purest gold."

"And a brain of cornmeal."

Even on horseback, Paley had trouble keepin up. As

they closed in on the others, Daniel could see them bunched up, old Cephus talking and gesturing. Flor scowled. "Would you like to bet a dollar on what he's talkin' about?"

Daniel said, "They won't pay any attention to him. Not Milo and them."

"Would you like to bet *two* dollars?"

Cephus kept up his intrigue all the way north, hunting out the men one at a time, except Daniel, for Daniel had made it plain enough where he stood. It seemed to him that Cephus spent an inordinate amount of time riding beside Milo Seldom, always talking as if his tongue were going to fall out tomorrow and he had to get all his say in now. Flor got to carrying her rifle across her lap.

They came eventually to an old cart road that ran east and west, weaving its way through the live-oak timbered hills, seeking out the easiest passages, though these had rough places that would jar loose a cart rider's teeth. Cephus Carmody pointed east. "Thataway," he said, "lies San Antonio." He turned and pointed northwest. "The road just goes a little ways, but where it plays out, and many days on past, is the San Saba mission."

Flor nodded, for she knew well enough what road this was. The country around San Antonio held few secrets for her. "All right, Papa, you lead us out."

"I'll lead, but *us* don't include you. We're goin' west; you're goin' east, daughter."

163

Flor's mouth went hard, and color surged into her cheeks. "Been expectin' this from you, Papa, but it won't work. This is my outfit, and these men are takin' orders from me."

Cephus braced his hands on the saddle and leaned back, his smiling face a picture of total confidence. "You think so, girl? Suppose you just ask them."

Flor cut a quick glance at Seldom. "Milo?"

Milo looked at the girl, but couldn't long face those sharp eyes. "Now, Flor, you got to give ol' Cephus credit for watchin' out after your safety. There ain't a one of us wants to see any harm come to you."

Flor saw her answer. She looked to Lalo Talavera. "Lalo?"

Lalo said in Spanish, "I have only respect for you, my little flower, and a warm spot for you in my heart. But a woman's place is in a man's kitchen or in his bed, not in his way."

Bitterly Flor said, "I never had much confidence in Milo, but I trusted you, Lalo."

"You can always trust me, little flower. I will see that your interests are protected. And sending you back to San Antonio will protect your person as well."

The Borrego brothers sat on their horses beside Lalo, and their apologetic shrugs showed they agreed with him. Armando said, "We shall see that you get your share of riches, Flor."

Flor saw that the other men were in agreement. All except Daniel and Paley Northcutt. Daniel said, "I'm with *you,* Flor." Paley said, "Me too, girl. Just tell me what you want me to do."

Cephus Carmody still grinned. "A man don't have to be smart with his ciphers to know whichaway the wind blows, daughter. You got one farmer and one drunk. Everybody else agrees with me. Now, this bein' a democracy and all, it looks to me like you're pretty badly outvoted."

Flor declared, "I ain't said nothin' about democracy. I'm still givin' the orders here, and there ain't no vote bein' taken." She swung the rifle up from her lap and pointed it at her father. "We're *all* goin' west, like we figured from the start."

Cephus looked at the huge bore, but he seemed not particularly disturbed. "Another thing about you, girl, you're unstable. Now, who do you think you're goin' to shoot with that thing? Me? You wouldn't shoot your old daddy; you love me too much. Anyway, if you *was* to shoot me, you wouldn't have nobody to point the way to that silver. And if you don't shoot me, there ain't no use in you shootin' anybody else, is there?"

Flor's knuckles were white on the rifle.

Daniel said sharply, "Maybe *she* wouldn't really shoot anybody, but I would."

Cephus cut him a look of sharp impatience. "Who? Pick you one." When Daniel did nothing, Cephus growled, "I swear, farmer, I wonder why you ever left the plow."

Milo Seldom said, "Friend Daniel, we're doin'

165

what's best for Flor. I'd sure be better suited if you didn't interfere."

Notchy O'Dowd pushed his horse up a little. "He ain't goin' to interfere," he said threateningly, his narrowed eyes on Daniel.

Angrily Daniel pushed his own horse forward to meet O'Dowd. Flor reached out to grab Daniel's arm. "He's just baitin' you, Daniel. There ain't nothin' you can do but get yourself whipped."

"It'd take some doin'," Daniel gritted.

"But he would do it. You want to come out of this with just one ear, like he's got?"

"What're we goin' to do, just give up?"

Flor let the rifle sag. "Looks like there's nothin' else we *can* do."

11

FLOR STOOD BESIDE HER HORSE, WATCHING THE MEN trail off leading the packmules, the dust slow to settle behind them in the hot stillness of the afternoon. She was saying nothing, but the set of her jaw indicated that if she did, it would not be fit for Christian ears to hear.

Bitterness churned in Daniel, reflecting on all he had gone through for a share of the silver, seeing it riding away and leaving him behind. "We could still catch up to them easy enough."

She turned on him. "And do what? They held all the cards, and they damn well knew it." The words were

English, but in her fury she lapsed into a bit of Mexican accent.

Daniel flinched at the sting of her anger. "At least they promised they'd bring you back a share of the silver."

"They got to find it first. You want to bet on them doin' that? The old man'll be so busy thinkin' how to cheat everybody else out of their share that he probably never will find that mine in the first place. Milo Seldom ain't got the judgment to find a silver mine if he fell down the shaft. And Lalo Talavera will have his mind on how many pretty women he can buy; he won't be much help findin' the place. The rest of them, all they can do is lead the mules."

Daniel shrugged. "Well, me and Paley'll see you safely to San Antonio."

"Who said I was goin' back?"

"Ain't you? What else can you do?"

"I can follow them. Sooner or later they're goin' to need somebody with a brain bigger than a buzzard egg."

Daniel frowned. "You mean you'd go out there by yourself? That's too dangerous."

"I'd hoped you'd go with me, Daniel."

He hadn't expected that. "I'd be pleasured, if you want me."

"If I didn't want you, I wouldn't of asked."

His glow at the invitation was so warm that he gave only a moment's thought to the danger and even the folly of what she suggested. "Sure, I'll go with you."

Paley Northcutt volunteered, "You can count on me, too."

167

Flor frowned, regret in her eyes. "No, Paley, I *can't* count on you."

Hurt came into Paley's flushed face. He looked at the ground, gathering his arguments. "Even if I wasn't half a man, I'd be *that* much help to you; and you know I'm a lot more than half a man. I been *much* of a man in my time."

Flor touched Paley's hand. "You're still a good man, Paley, at heart. But you know you're undependable. We'd be worryin' about you instead of watchin' out for the needful things."

"There ain't no whisky out there, Flor. You know it's the whisky makes me thataway."

"But the cravin' after whisky could be as bad on you as the drinkin' of it. What if we got out there a hundred miles by ourselves and you started to come apart?"

"I wouldn't, Flor. I promise you, I wouldn't."

Flor stared up at him, her anger gone and sorrow taking its place. "You know I wouldn't hurt you for all the world, Paley, if there wasn't no need. But there's no use talkin'. You can't go; we can't afford you."

Paley looked to Daniel for help. Daniel said, "Flor, maybe if—" He stopped then, for her look told him there was no use going on with it, and he sensed that she was right. Better a little hurt for Paley now than the risk of disaster somewhere out in the unknown.

Flor said, "You go on back to town."

Paley hung his head. "You know I don't want to.

168

You know what I'll do when I get there; I'll find me a jug and a sleepin' place in some alley."

Flor looked away from him. "I'm sorry, Paley. If you push, you can make it by dark."

Paley sadly accepted the judgment. "How you-all figure to eat? They didn't have leave you nothin'."

Daniel blinked, for he hadn't even thought of that. In her anger, Flor evidently hadn't either. "We'll manage."

Paley Northcutt rode east down the cart road, looking back over his shoulder as if hoping they would relent. Daniel suspected Flor wanted to, but she sternly held her ground. After a while Paley was out of sight in the live-oak timber. Daniel said, "Reckon we'd better be goin' too."

"We'll wait awhile. They may be lookin' for us to follow them. We can always track them later; I expect they'll leave a trail like the Mexican army, that damned ol' Cephus."

Daniel swung down from the saddle and seated himself against the heavy trunk of a big live oak, the dry leaves from past seasons like a mat beneath him. "I never heard anybody talk about their daddy the way you do. Don't think much of him, do you?"

Flor sat down beside him, holding the reins. Daniel found the nearness of her aroused him a little. She said, "I suppose I talk rougher than I really feel. I love him in a way, and yet again I get so disgusted with him I could shoot him."

"Maybe it's like he says—maybe he's just thinkin' of your best interests."

"He may be my daddy, but he'd cheat me out of my own burial money if he could figure a scheme. If he found a whole mountain of silver out there—more money than he could spend in ten lifetimes—he'd still try to do me out of my share. That's why I got to be there. If he does find that silver and I'm not with him, I'll never see him again this side of hell."

"Milo Seldom wouldn't let him cheat you."

"Milo Seldom would probably lose his share too if he ever turned his back on that old reprobate. Milo's not a bad sort, but he's got a trustin' nature, like you. When they passed out the brains, he was off huntin' somethin' to eat."

Daniel considered a while, then decided to probe. "Milo has a notion you're in love with him."

She laughed aloud. "Me, with that backwoods tramp, the seat hangin' out of his britches?" She shook her head. "I'll admit there was a time that I sort of had a feelin' towards him. That was till I knew better, till I saw how much he was like my ol' daddy—restless, no-account, keepin' what he ought to throw away, throwin' away what he ought to keep. Only difference between him and Cephus is that he ain't dishonest. Devious, sometimes, but not dishonest."

Daniel frowned. "The way you hollered for somebody to pull him out of the Rio Grande, I thought maybe . . ."

"I'd of done as much for a spotted dog."

Daniel poked at the leaves with a stick he had picked up. "I'm glad to know how you really feel."

"It makes that much difference to you?"

"It might."

He found her studying him intently, smiling a little. His first thought was that she might be laughing at him, but he decided that was not true. She simply said, "Daniel, I like you."

The smile didn't promise anything, and he wasn't asking, not yet. It was enough that she smiled.

They had sat there awhile when Flor nudged him. She pointed and whispered, "We were wonderin' how we'd eat. The Lord always provides." Daniel saw a fat doe grazing at the edge of an open grassy spot, where two good bounds would carry her back into the cover of a live-oak motte. The doe had probably seen the horses but was used to the wild ones which roamed this western country. Daniel carefully pushed to his feet, bringing up his rifle and moving cautiously to get clear of the horses before he fired. It would be no accomplishment if he bagged their supper but ran off their horses.

The doe dropped at the first shot, and he used his hunting knife to finish the work of the rifle. In a little while he had the hindquarters, the hide still on them, and the backstrap. Flor kindled a fire and drove a couple of forked sticks into the ground. She cut some of the backstrap into strips and wrapped them around a long stick, then laid the stick across the forks as the fire died down.

"Least they could've done was to've left us some coffee," she complained. "But they figured we'd make San Antonio by night."

171

"What do you think they'll say when they find out we've followed them?"

"We won't show ourselves till we're too far out there for them to turn us back." An expression of pleased malice came into her face. "With Cephus and Milo tryin' to lead them, they'll be in trouble and glad to see us."

The venison was done eventually, and they ate aplenty. Flor said her father and other frontiersmen of the wandering kind always ate heartily when they had it, on the assumption it might be a long wait until the next time. She broiled some more to pack for cold camp tomorrow. This done, they rode awhile. Presently Daniel glanced back over his shoulder and saw a moving figure far behind them. Flor squinted and cursed a little in Spanish. "That damned Paley Northcutt. Him followin' us, us followin' them. This is a silly situation."

They rode by a live-oak motte, cut back into it from the far side and stepped down from the horses to wait until Paley came even with them. When he did, Flor cut loose and gave him a shameless cussing that no one could have failed to understand.

Paley hung his head. "Thought I might be able to help."

"Go on back to San Antonio," she told him sharply. "That'll be the biggest help."

Paley turned around. This time, Daniel thought, he would keep going.

When Paley was well out of sight, Daniel and Flor

172

rode again, following the plain tracks. Daniel kept his gaze sweeping the land in front of them, frequently turning, however, to look behind them. He did not really expect to find hostile Indians here, for they had not been seen this near San Antonio in a long time; but Indians were always doing what you didn't expect them to. If they had always followed a pattern like civilized people, Daniel thought, they wouldn't have been so damned much trouble.

Despite their long wait and the time they took fixing and eating a meal, Daniel found by the fresh horse and mule sign that he and Flor were catching up to Cephus' and Milo's party. The two backwoodsmen seemed in no big rush to get at that silver.

"Savin' the horses," Daniel surmised.

"Savin' theirselves," Flor corrected him. "They ain't either one of them partial to sweat."

The sun went down, though the south wind continued to carry the remnant of its heat as the bright cherry-red of the clouds dulled to purple in the west. "They'll be makin' camp about now," Flor said. "I'd like to be where I could see their fire. We can make ourselves a cold camp."

Daniel was so intent on looking for sign of fire ahead that he didn't see Cephus and Notchy O'Dowd ride out of a cedar thicket until it was too late to do anything but meet them head on. Cephus looked hurt. "Daughter, it grieves me that you don't take an order from your old daddy any more. I told you as plain as I knew how. It shames me in front of my friends for my daughter to disobey me thisaway."

"Obedience ain't in my nature, Papa. I'm that much like you."

Cephus turned his attention to Daniel. "Boy, didn't your folks teach you to obey your elders?"

"Some elders," Daniel said stiffly.

Notchy O'Dowd got down from his horse and moved toward Flor. "What this girl of yours needs, Cephus, is a good beatin' to remind her of her upbringin'." He made as if to reach for her and found himself staring into the bore of her rifle.

"You touch me," she said evenly, "and there'll be another hole in your head bigger than your mouth."

Cephus pulled his horse up closer. "Now, Notchy, ain't no need of hurtin' this little girl; a gentle talkin'-to is all she needs." He got close enough to grab the rifle barrel and give it a quick twist. Flor cried out in surprise and pain. Cephus had the rifle by then, and Flor was rubbing her hurt hand.

Notchy reached up and grabbed Daniel, jerking him out of the saddle. "A little lesson might be good for this farmer, though." Before Daniel could get to his feet, O'Dowd hit him in the face with his big fist. Daniel stumbled and went down on his back. He saw O'Dowd dive at him, and managed to roll over so that the man's whole weight didn't crush him. He lost half his breath, though, even as it was. He hit O'Dowd in the mouth and drew blood, but he sensed that he wasn't giving half as much as he was taking.

The anger surged up in him, and the hard muscles

that came from farm work and guiding a plow. He got a few deep breaths to bring his strength back, then shoved O'Dowd aside so that he was able to gain his feet. When O'Dowd rushed him, the man ran into a fist as hard as a cedar knot. Daniel saw surprise as well as pain in the bloody face. He saw O'Dowd's mutilated ear and remembered what Milo had told him of this man's reputation as a brawler. It came to Daniel that O'Dowd when aroused could kill a man if given a chance. Daniel did not intend to give him one. He took a hard blow to his stomach, but in trade gave O'Dowd another taste of knuckles in the mouth. While O'Dowd faltered, Daniel swung again, catching him squarely in the right eye. It would be awhile before O'Dowd saw much through that one, Daniel thought.

O'Dowd reached down to his boot and came up with a knife. Daniel's heart jumped, and so did he as O'Dowd savagely slashed at him. The man missed by a good margin and, overextended, went down on one knee. This gave Daniel time to look around for something to use against him. He came up with a dried cedar branch. When O'Dowd tried once more to come at him, Daniel cracked it over his head. It sounded like a shot. O'Dowd went down as if it had been one.

Cephus looked ruefully at the fallen man. "Notchy," he said, "I believe you've done enough to this farmer boy. Let's let him go this time and not hurt him no more if he'll promise to behave himself."

O'Dowd raged helplessly, pushing up onto hands

and knees and trying vainly to see Daniel. One eye was swollen shut, and sweat and dirt rolled into the other, blinding him. Cephus helped O'Dowd stagger to his feet and guided him to his horse. O'Dowd summoned strength to get into the saddle, cursing with every breath. Cephus turned back to his daughter and Daniel. "I hope this'll be a lesson to both of you. Don't you be followin' us no more. I'd hate to see this happen again."

Flor was immensely pleased. "I'll bet you would."

"You go on back to San Antonio now, do you hear me?"

"I hear you, Papa."

"You promise?"

"I promise."

Satisfied, Cephus rode on, leading O'Dowd's horse. It was all O'Dowd could do to stay up there.

Daniel rubbed his face and found blood on his hand. He looked at Flor in surprise. "I didn't think you'd promise a thing like that."

"Another thing I learned from my ol' daddy. I lie." She smiled. "We crossed a little stream back yonder. Let's go wash you up a little."

He lay on his stomach and cupped his hands, bringing the cool water up to his cut and bruised face. It felt good. When he was satisfied that the blood was gone, he turned over and pushed to his feet, wiping his face on his sleeve. Flor motioned for him to sit down beside a nearby live oak, and explored his face, then his hands with her gentle fingers.

"You came out a sight better than O'Dowd," she said. "I don't see anything here that ought to even leave a scar." She had cut a little tallow from the deer, and she rubbed this into the wounds. "That ought at least make it feel better."

"It feels good anyway," he said. "You know, I won that fight."

"Sure you did. You got more strength than even you knew about, Daniel. You're *muy macho* when you need to be."

It occurred to Daniel that he had never had to prove himself back in Hopeful Valley. He had never really known how he would react when the binding got tight. Thanks to Milo Seldom and this trip, he had had several chances to find out. For that, at least, he owed Milo.

She said, "I believe you're pleased with yourself."

"Matter of fact, I am. I never much favored a man that bragged, but I can't help feelin' thisaway."

"You earned it." Touching his cheek with the palm of her hand, she stared at him a moment, then leaned forward and gently kissed him. He was surprised, but not so much so that he let the gesture go unanswered. He brought his arms around her and pulled her tight. Her hands went to his back, pressing hard. Suddenly the kiss was no longer gentle, it was hungry and urgent. The fire came up in him, and he sensed that her cheeks flushed warm.

She said, "I don't believe you've ever held a woman this way."

He had held Lizbeth, but not quite like this.

She said, "Well, you're doin' all right. Don't quit now."

Her arms tightened around him, and he knew he wasn't going to stop here where he had always stopped with Lizbeth. He couldn't have now, even if he had wanted to.

12

THEY HAD BUILT NO FIRE. THEY LAY ON THEIR BLANkets by the little stream, listening to the crickets and the insistent calling of the night birds, staring up through the blackness of the overhanging live oak to the sparkling stars that shone through in the thin spots. Daniel said, "The more I think about it, the more I admit it's a long-shot idea, us trailin' after them thisaway. Two of us by ourselves won't be no match for any Indians we come across."

"All the tracks them others are makin', if the Indians find anybody it'll be *them*. They won't expect two more followin' way behind. If we're watchful, we won't be seen."

Daniel shrugged. "A big chance, even for all that silver."

"No chance is too big for what that silver could buy us."

"What'll it buy *you,* Flor? All I've heard you talk about is silk and velvet dresses. I don't see how a dress could mean that much."

"It's not the dresses, really; they're just what you put up front to show. It's what the dresses stand for—money, respectability."

"Money don't mean the same as respectability. I've seen folks that had money but wasn't respectable."

"But didn't people pretend like they was, and bow and scrape?"

Daniel admitted they did.

"When I wear them silk dresses around the plazas of San Antonio, people will know I'm not just some half-breed girl that washes other folks' dirty clothes and that they suspicion of doin' God knows what else to make herself a livin'. They'll know I'm somebody, that I got more money than *they* have. They'll look up to me instead of down."

"People must've mistreated you pretty bad, Flor."

"The *Americanos,* they look down on me for my Mexican blood. The Mexicans, they look down on me for my American blood. Besides, they know damn well who my ol' daddy is. If you think Americans know how to insult somebody, you ought to see an aristocratic Mexican do it; they've made it a science. You ain't been properly put down into your rightful place till you've had it done to you by some pure-blood *gachupín.* They've handled peons for two hundred years."

The bitterness was strong in her voice, and Daniel began to get some idea of how lonely a life she had led, half of one culture, half of another, not really belonging to either one. He took her hand. "To hell

179

with people that hurt you. I'd just go somewhere else."

"If I get me a share of that silver, I'll go someplace, but first I want to rub those people's faces in it a little."

"You ever think about livin' on a farm, Flor?"

"I've thought about it. A farmer can be as poor as anybody else."

"But never hungry. They can't starve a good farmer to death because he can always grow somethin' to eat. I may not know a lot of other things, but I'm a good farmer."

"You tryin' to ask me to marry you, Daniel?"

The thought startled him. "Maybe I am. Maybe I was by way of workin' up to it gradual."

"Well, don't; not now. I ain't sure yet just what I want."

Daniel frowned. "Maybe I misunderstood. While ago I thought . . ."

"While ago I did what I felt like doin' right then. I'm not ready to decide what I'll want to do the rest of my life."

"You keep on thinkin' about it, anyway, and remember that I've asked you."

Though Texans usually spoke of anything beyond the settlements as being "west," the San Saba mission and *presidio* had actually been built as much north as west of San Antonio de Bexar. The Spaniards had set up the mission to convert the Apache Indians about the

180

middle 1700's, and had built a stone fortress just across the river to protect the mission. It did not do its job. Comanches, enemies of the Apaches in those days, viewed the project as an insult and sacked the mission, leaving it a blazing ruin, priests and Indian converts lying dead in their smoky wake. The garrison remained for several years, with its soldiers uneasy and ineffective, but men of the cross never returned.

The way to the *presidio* had been well mapped during the years of its service, but few white men now living had ever visited there. It was said that Jim Bowie had paused to carve his name upon the crumbling stones at the entrance.

It seemed to Daniel that Milo and Cephus were taking a lot of time and not making many miles; once they paused half a day just to hunt buffalo from among the several herds through which they passed. Though one would have furnished them all the meat they needed, they had left twenty dead buffalo behind them, strung out for two miles. They had cut into most of the carcasses only to the extent necessary to retrieve their lead for remolding into bullets; lead was hard to come by, and not to be wasted.

"Chased them on horseback," Daniel observed.

Flor said disgustedly, "Like kids, only this ain't no place for kids. Where there's this many buffalo, there's apt to be Indians."

The meat from the fat doe had not been enough to last long. They had decided against firing a rifle and drawing the attention of either friends or foes. Daniel had tried unsuccessfully the last couple of nights to locate a wild-turkey roost or to catch a rabbit in a snare. Under the shade of a big mesquite tree they came across a young buffalo cow, wounded in the foreshoulder and left to die.

"The wolves'll get her if we don't," Daniel said.

"I don't know how we can get her without shootin' her."

Daniel rode up close. Maddened by pain, the cow charged. But fevering and loss of blood had left her weak. She fell to one knee, staying there awhile, slinging her head before she mustered enough strength to regain her feet. Daniel rode in close again, circling slowly so that she kept having to turn to face him in her anger. He began moving faster, so that she had to turn faster too. Inevitably she lost her footing and went down. Daniel jumped to the ground, unsheathed his knife and plunged it into her throat, stepping back to avoid the sharp horns as she slung her head. She almost got up, then sank. In a little while she was dead.

Daniel examined the swollen wound and decided against taking meat from that area or the hump for fear of infection. He cut off the hindquarters, leaving the hide in place.

He didn't like the way he had had to kill the cow, but Flor pointed out that the wolves would have begun eating her while she still lived. "She's out of her misery now, and we may just be startin' ours." Flor worried. "If there's an Indian in twenty miles, all that shootin' and chasin' after buffalo is likely to've drawn him. By now they probably know about Milo and Cephus and them others, if they didn't before. We'd best do our travelin' by night and shade up in the day-time."

She made it as a positive statement, not asking for advice. Daniel said, "I doubt we can follow them tracks at night, even in the bright moonlight. There's too much grass on the ground."

Impatiently Flor demanded, "You sayin' I'm wrong?"

"I say you're wrong."

She stiffened, not used to being argued with. "Well, we'll try it my way. I don't fancy havin' my hair hang in some tepee for an ornament."

They rode on, following the tracks a few more miles, then turned off into a heavy live-oak motte to build a tiny fire and cook their meat while there was yet daylight to hide the blaze. Any Indian who caught and followed the smoke smell would find only ashes, for Flor and Daniel would put the spot far behind them. The stop for cooking had given the horses a rest, so they pushed on into the dusk, and then into dark-ness.

The horsemen ahead of them followed a fairly straight course. But even so, in the first hour of dark-ness Daniel lost the trail. He and Flor both got off their horses and searched afoot for sign. They lost an hour or more.

At length Flor said sharply, "Go ahead and say it."

183

"Say what?"

"Say you told me so."

"I don't have to, now."

Angrily she said, "You'd better not."

Eventually it was Daniel who found the trace. He came upon droppings left by a horse or mule. On hands and knees he was able to tell where the hoofs had bruised and bent the grass. But following this thin trace in the moonlight was a slow process. In daylight they could get the trail's course and pick some distant landmark toward which the trail seemed to run. They could then make good time, pausing only now and again to be sure they hadn't lost the tracks. In the night, distant landmarks could not be seen. They followed awhile, but soon lost the tracks again.

Flor grumbled.

Daniel asked, "What did you say?"

"You wouldn't want to hear it. I was cussin' myself. It hurts to be wrong, and have the other person know it."

"I'm makin' no issue of it."

"You should. What do you think we ought to do?"

"Make a cold camp, set out again at first light."

"All right. We tried it my way; now we'll try it yours."

If they had been wary in traveling before, they were even more so now. They would try to determine the direction of the trail, then follow it in only a general way, holding to cedar and oak timber for cover as much as they could. Once in a while when they could follow a live-oak ridge down close to where they thought the trail would be, they would ride out and be sure they were still paralleling it. Always they found the tracks there, about where they were expecting them.

They stopped about midafternoon to cook up some more of the buffalo meat, careful to use only dry wood that would not put up much smoke, keeping the fire as small as was possible for it to do the job. Waiting, they watched a small armadillo digging for grubs at the edge of the motte, its high-curved shell looking like a suit of armor. Daniel pointed. "You ever watch an armadillo, really *watch* one?"

Flor shook her head. "Never was all that curious."

"Folks claim that when they have a litter, all the babies are the same—either all males or all female. They don't come mixed up."

Flor frowned, then a light of humor came into her eyes, the first he had seen in a while. "Sounds risky to me. What if the averages didn't work out? What if all the armadillos started havin' just one or the other? Wouldn't take long for things to get in an awful mess."

Daniel shrugged. "I reckon you just have to trust Nature to take care of things like that."

Flor put her arms around Daniel. "I'll trust Nature. She's always been pretty good to *me*."

Daniel had spent the larger part of his life in the gentle valleys and rolling hills along the lower Colorado River. The rocky limestone hills and now and again the big up-thrusts of red granite in this higher

185

and drier land looked like mountains to him; they were the tallest he had ever seen. Times, in the early morning or late afternoon, those in the distance took on a deep blue or purple appearance, and a fine haze clung about them, giving them a ghostly look that sent shivers up his spine. Times he felt like an invader, going where the Lord had never intended him to go, reaching for things the Lord had not intended him to have, disturbing an ageless peace, an alien land reserved for another people.

He and Flor saw deer aplenty, and doves and quail and wild turkey. Once they saw a black bear, its rolling gait carrying it up a hillside into a heavy cedar thicket. Clear streams murmured over limestone rocks at frequent intervals; cool clean water from tiny springs which broke out of the layered ledges at a thousand places.

No wonder, he thought, this beautiful, bounteous land had long been jealously guarded by various Indian tribes against one another, against the Spaniards, against the Mexicans and now against the venturesome *Americanos*. It gave him an awesome feeling to know that few men of his own kind had yet been where he now rode. The time would come, he knew, when white men would move here as they had moved into every other Indian land so far. They would take this land and put their plows into the deep soil of these broad flats, graze their cattle on the hills, build their houses over the cold ashes of Indian camp-grounds. He wondered if any would ever know that he—Daniel Provost—had passed this way; if in any way he would leave a lasting mark on this land.

One day he and Flor came upon horsetracks, cutting diagonally across the course they were following in an effort to parallel Cephus and Milo. This new set of tracks led directly down to intercept those of the Texan silver hunters. It could have been wild horses, Daniel thought, though somehow he knew it was not.

"How many?" Flor asked him with concern.

Daniel shook his head. "Can't say for sure. Five or six."

"Well, that's not enough to jump Milo."

"It's enough to follow along and spy on them until they get a big enough bunch together." Daniel sat at the edge of the live oaks that hid him and Flor, his narrowed eyes worriedly studying the course the Indian tracks took and calculating about where they would cross that other trail. "You stay here. I'm takin' a chance and ridin' down there. It's possible the Indians came along before Cephus and Milo."

Flor stayed, nervously watching for sign of Indians, while Daniel gave the whole area a good scrutiny, cinched up his courage and rode down into the flat, where he was in broad open country except for a thin scattering of single mesquite trees. When he saw no sign of Indians, he eased a little. He followed the new tracks until they intersected the others. He swore under his breath as he saw that the Indians had come after the other party. The red men had milled around, evidently studying their discovery. One had ridden off at a northerly angle. The rest of the Indian tracks merged into those of the first group. Daniel looked around for a few minutes, then rode back to Flor.

"They're followin' Milo," he said. "They sent one man off; I expect he's gone to report to others some-place."

Alarmed, Flor said, "I hope Milo and them have got sense enough to keep awake, and not get caught by surprise."

Daniel nodded. "I think they know *that* much. Me and you, Flor, we better not both be asleep at the same time, either." He started on, moving northwesterly but taking even more pains now to stay in or near the cover of live oak and cedar. When they had to move across the open, they paused and took careful appraisal of the land around them.

As they had done before, they moved in the day-time, pausing once to cook up some meat, and kept moving until dark. The next night, dusk caught them in rough hills where rocky ground made the trail much harder to follow. For long stretches, fresh droppings were almost the only discernible sign. Daniel was almost ready to call a halt when suddenly in the moon-light he saw the ground drop away in front of him. Far below he saw a dark mass of timber and the silver sheen of a broad, winding river. He started to push for-ward, but the horse balked. Then Daniel realized that he had ridden out almost to the edge of a rimrock. He pulled the roan back quickly.

"Flor, that's no little creek down yonder. We've

already crossed the Guadalupe and the Llano. That'd have to be the San Saba, wouldn't it?" He tried to sound matter-of-fact, but the realization brought a prickling to him, and a sudden impatience. Out yonder somewhere lay a fortune in unclaimed silver, or so people said. He started looking for a way down around the rimrock, but then he reined up, raising his hand. Across the river and some distance upstream—he couldn't tell how far—he saw a reddish dot of fire-light.

Flor saw it too. "Is it Cephus' camp, or is it Indians?"

"I'm not in no hurry to go and find out." So far as he could tell, the little trailing party of Indians had crossed over the river in the wake of the treasure hunters. "I say the smart thing for us to do is stay on this side till it comes daylight and we can see the lay of the land. Otherwise we're liable to ride in on a bunch of Indians like a fly hittin' a spiderweb."

Flor followed without question as he backed away from the edge and sought cover behind the hill. It occurred to Daniel that in these long days and nights of traveling together she had begun looking to him for leadership rather than giving orders as she had done before. Up to now, at least, his leadership had not brought them into any trouble.

They backtracked a hundred yards or so from this side of the bank, where the footing was easier, and began working their way along. Daniel chose grassy ground where the horses' hoofs would not strike against rocks and make noise that might carry to the other side. At length they were about even with the fire. Daniel dismounted and led his horse into a cluster of timber to tie it. He moved afoot toward the bank. He did not have to look back to know that Flor was close behind him.

He could see the fire now, though the flames had died down to a soft red glow that put out too little light to reveal what was around it. A figure moved on the near side, but the distance was too great for Daniel to see any detail, and the glimpse was all too brief. He had no idea whether the man was white or Indian.

In the moonlight he got the impression of some large dark shadow, like a line of heavy brush perhaps, the glow in the middle of it.

Flor said, "If that's Cephus and Milo, it might be a good time to get down to them, to let them know the Indians are trailin' them."

"How we goin' to get down there without maybe runnin' into them Indians ourselves? I think we'd best hold onto what we got."

Flor accepted his judgment without argument. They sat there without thought of sleeping, watching that fire die away and the glow fade into darkness. Sometime toward morning Daniel felt Flor's weight go slack against his arm. Gently he moved her so that she lay with her head in his lap. She slept quietly, but he never did. He kept watching the point where the fire had been, trying to figure out the heavy dark shadow which seemed gradually to change in the night as the moon moved.

The moon went down, and it was dark a long time before the first light of morning began in the east, and the long shadows began to draw back toward the big pecan trees and the gnarled live oaks along the river. As dawn gradually came, Daniel watched the place where he had seen the fire. Slowly it became clear what the heavy shadows had been in the moonlight. He could see stone walls, high in places, badly crumbled in others. A chill ran up his back. His voice was shaky with excitement. "Flor, that's the San Saba *presidio*."

Flor blinked, then raised up, suddenly awake. She grabbed Daniel's hand. "We *did* make it."

"You ever doubt it?"

"Followin' my ol' daddy? You damn bet you I doubted it."

In broadening daylight Daniel could see men begin to stir, and he saw the familiar packmules staked within the protection of the walls. "That's them. I can see Milo; I can tell him even from here."

"How? Did he fall over his own feet, or somethin'?"

"We could ride down there now and they couldn't hardly run us off any more. But I'd sure like to know where them Indians are at." He realized that if he could see the men at the fortress, he could be seen too. He stretched out on his belly. He let his gaze slowly work up and down the river, through the heavy green foliage, along the riverbank. Then he saw the Indians.

"Yonder, scattered amongst them big pecan trees."

Flor saw. "Wish we could go warn Milo."

"With them Indians between us, we'd better not even try."

Flor shook her head and mumbled a few cuss words. "Look at them *ladrones* down there fixin' themselves a hot breakfast. God, what I'd give for somethin' besides a chunk of dried buffalo."

It was an hour or more before the men inside the *presidio* walls began throwing packs on the mules and saddling their horses. Daniel saw Milo Seldom pour something out of a bucket near the campfire and knew it was coffee. "Damn his wasteful soul," he muttered. "Wisht I could make him eat that, grounds and all."

The men rode out the gates, bringing up the pack-mules. Daniel could see Cephus taking the lead, sitting proud in his saddle, still wearing that stolen Mexican uniform, gesturing importantly so that everyone should realize his position of leadership; he was the man who would shortly make them rich. Twenty or thirty yards outside the gate, Cephus halted his horse and carefully looked around, getting his bearings. He pointed north and a little east, then led the way up a gentle slope that seemed to promise a gentler, more even stretch of rolling hills.

Flor said disgustedly, "Puffed up like a toad, and them others makin' over him like he was the king of Sheba."

"At least he knows where the silver is at. I wisht we was down there with them."

"We got one advantage. We know where the Indians are."

"Lot of good that'll do us if they get to the mine and we're stuck up here on this high hill."

"I don't think I ever heard Cephus say how long a ride it is from the ruins to the mine—whether it's a mile or a hundred miles. All I know is that he said he had to start at the *presidio* to find it."

"If there's as much silver as they say, they can't load it all up and get away in a hurry. We'll catch up to them."

"Yeah, and maybe them Indians will, too."

The treasure party disappeared over the hill. When they were well out of sight, Daniel saw activity among the pecan trees in the river bed. Five men, all but naked, rode out taking their time.

"Reckon what they are?" Daniel mused. "Comanche, Apache or what?"

Flor shrugged. "*Quién sabe?* Indians come in two kinds: friendly and hostile. I'd hate to depend on that bunch for friendship."

Daniel watched the Indians leisurely take up the trail. They were a wild and barbaric sight to him, fascinating and yet somehow chilling. "It *is* their country," he said. "Come right down to it, we got no business here."

"I got more use for that silver than they have," Flor replied. "That silver is all I want from this country. They can keep the rest of it."

"Once white men get the silver, they'll come for the land itself."

Daniel itched to move down the hill when the Indians were out of sight and cross the river to examine the ruins. But he held himself back. There could be more Indians down there that he had not seen. He lay on the hilltop and stared a long time at the rock walls, trying to reconstruct them in his mind, peopling them with Spanish soldiers and mentally placing cannons on the four round corner towers. He knew from stories that the mission was supposed to have been on the opposite side of the river and that the Comanches had bypassed the *presidio* to attack the more vulnerable churchyard.

If any sign of the mission was left, he could not see it from here. But he could make out what appeared to be an irrigation ditch, angling away from a small man-made dam that lay partially ruined by floodwaters. The ditch led to what he judged could have been tilled fields.

"Longer I look at it," he said, "more it looks to me like this must've been a mighty poor place. Livin' was hard, them days. They didn't have none of our modern convenience."

"I don't expect they did."

"If they had all that silver, how come they lived so poor?"

Flor offered no answer.

After a long time they still had seen no sign of more Indians. Daniel said, "We just as well be movin'." He led the way around the rimrock and down to an easy ford which he judged had probably been used between the *presidio* and the mission. The fortress lay just up

194

the bank, barely past the floodline. The half-tumbled walls brought an unexpected shiver to Daniel as he mentally pushed back the years to a time even before his father had been born. He wondered how many Spaniards had died here and lay buried somewhere out yonder in a lonely, lost graveyard, hundreds of miles from their own kind.

"Place kind of makes my back crawl," he complained.

Flor hoped to find some supplies that the hunters might carelessly have left behind them, but there was not a thing except one worn-out moccasin, a ragged hole in its sole. "Milo Seldom's from the size of it," she gritted. "He's got a foot like a draft horse."

She's sure ridin' ol' Milo hard, Daniel thought. But he guessed she had reason. He reminded her that Milo had been wearing boots.

He looked at carvings on the rock at the front gate. He made out the names of Padilla and Cos and remembered there had been a Mexican general named Cos with Santa Anna in the big war. Then he found the name he sought: Bowie.

Up to now all the Bowie stories had been just that—*stories.* But these crudely carved letters were a reality, something he could see, something he could trace with his forefinger.

His skin prickled, and of a sudden he could almost see that silver—could almost taste it on his tongue.

"Let's go, Flor," he said impatiently. "That mine is out yonder, just waitin' for us."

13

THEY USED MUCH THE SAME TACTICS TRAILING MILO and Cephus as they had used the last few days, but now the brush cover was scantier as the country changed into gentler rolling hills. There were long stretches when Daniel and Flor had no choice but to risk riding out in the wide open. After a few times they eased considerably, but they rode with rifles across their laps, primed and ready.

After two or three hours Daniel found they had lost the track, trying to parallel it rather than follow it directly. He spent an hour searching, Flor moving out well to one side and helping him hunt. When finally he picked up the trail he found that the horsemen had altered direction.

Daniel suggested, "Likely ol' Cephus picked him out a fresh landmark." Offhand he could not see exactly what. He spotted a couple of hills in the line of march, but they looked about like all the others.

They moved off to one side of the trail again where there was at least partial cover. Now and then a deer bounded off for timber. A chaparral hawk or *paisano* would sprint out of their path, building up speed and taking off to soar low across the open prairie. When Daniel decided it would be a good idea to check the trail again, it was not where it was supposed to be. Backtracking, he found the tracks leading off in a ninety-degree angle from their former course.

"Followin' another landmark," Daniel said.

Flor grunted. "Or followin' shadows. You don't know that old badger the way I do."

This time Daniel decided that if they were not to lose Milo and Cephus altogether, they would have to abandon any attempt at following the cover and just stay with the tracks. The cover didn't amount to much anyway, except sporadically.

"This runs up the odds that we'll be seen," Flor countered.

"The odds of not losin' that bunch go even higher if we don't change our ways. It comes down to a question of how bad we want that silver."

"You know the answer to that; otherwise there wouldn't neither one of us be here."

They moved cautiously across the sun-cured grass of the deep live-oak and mesquite flats, up the gentle but rocky hills, careful never to top out against a skyline if there were any other way to go. Now and again they encountered buffalo in groups of five or ten or twenty, shaggy dark beasts which edged away from the horses, for they knew what it was to be chased by bow-and-arrow hunters. Daniel had a hard time, sometimes, pulling his eyes away from the buffalo and searching the area ahead of them for sign of Indians. He had never seen many buffalo before; not many ranged down into the settled country such as Hopeful Valley any more.

"You ever see such a country for grass?" he asked, half in awe. "Drier than at home, but I bet it's sure got the strength in it. Look at them buffalo and then imagine what a man could do grazin' this country with cattle."

"First thing he'd do," Flor said, "would be to lose his hair."

"I'm not talkin' about now. The Indians can't hold it forever, not a rich-lookin' grazin' country like this. Somebody'll bring cows here one of these days, and all the Indians in a hundred miles won't run him off of this good grass."

"I'm not concerned with what's on top of the ground; I'm wantin' to get what's under it. Give me a muleload of silver and you can have all the grass from here to Kingdom Come."

Daniel said, "I bet this'd be good country for farmin', too, if it ever gets enough rain. Man, I'd like to drop a plow into one of these pretty flats."

"If there's as much silver as they claim, you'll have money enough that you won't have to drop a plow no-place unless you want to."

"I'll want to. Sure, it gets tiresome sometimes, but it takes hold of a man. If he ever gets it deep in his system, I doubt that he'll ever get it plumb out."

He reined up as the trail suddenly veered once more, almost due east this time. Daniel could tell by the tracks that the animals had milled around a good while here. He studied the skyline with sharp curiosity. "Cephus must've picked him a new landmark. But I wonder what it was?"

He saw nothing outstanding. Some hills lay yonderway, but they all looked pretty much alike, and they were little different from those he saw to the north and west, or along their backtrail. "I reckon maybe Cephus knows what he's doin'."

"I'd hate to bet my life on it," Flor said, then considered. "But I am; we *all* are."

They rode perhaps an hour, following this new direction. The droppings were fresher now, so Daniel knew he and Flor were catching up. He began worrying how they could join Milo and Cephus without running headlong into those trailing Indians.

He heard a drumming sound and reined up abruptly, looking back. Flor heard it too. "Horse," she said, "runnin'."

"Horses," he corrected her, "a bunch of them." He hadn't seen them yet, which meant he and Flor probably hadn't been seen either. "We better do some runnin' ourselves. There's a right smart of timber over yonderway." He heeled his horse into a lope, looking back to be sure Flor was with him. She was. He took to rocky ground at first in hopes they wouldn't leave tracks that might be noticed. After a hundred yards or so he quit the rocks and went straight for the live-oak cover.

They had hardly reached it when he saw horsemen break out into an open flat. At this distance he couldn't count, but there must have been twenty or more, maybe even thirty. He stepped down and covered his horse's nose to make sure the animal didn't nicker to the other horses.

Flor was paling a little. It was one thing to talk bravely in San Antonio; it was something else to be out here in the midst of this unknown country, looking death in the eye. She started to say something, swallowed and stayed silent. Her wide eyes said it all.

Daniel brought his longrifle up across his left arm, cradling it for quick use. His hands trembled a little, and he found himself fervently wishing he were back in Hopeful Valley, following that plow and staring into the prosaic rear of that old brown mule Hezekiah. Why in the hell had he talked himself into coming on a wild mission like this? All the silver in Texas wouldn't do a man any good if he were lying in the sun with his glazed eyes open and his scalp gone.

The Indians held their course, loping their horses easily across the open grass. In following the plain trail left by Cephus and Milo and the others, they never saw Daniel and Flor take out for the timber. At one point they came close enough for Daniel to see the feathers in their hair and the colored designs painted on the hard bullhide shields they carried. He saw the bois d'arc bows and the feathered shafts in the quivers against their backs.

The Indians were long gone before Daniel's dry mouth worked up saliva enough for him to swallow and clear his throat for speaking. He said foolishly, "Did you see that?"

She said something under her breath and added, "I hope Milo has got his eyes open." She held out her hand and found it shaking. "What do we do now?"

Daniel did not consider long. "The Indians went thataway." He pointed. "I think we ought to go this-away. We can still move in the same general direction but keep a hill or two between us and them."

"What if Cephus changes direction again?"

"Damn him, he'd just better not."

They had to ride two miles or more in a tangent before they found a saddle in the hill and could ride up over it to regain more or less their original direction. Moving down the far side, Daniel halted awhile and dismounted to study the land below them. He spent ten or fifteen minutes before he was satisfied that nothing moved except a few buffalo. Their presence convinced him there weren't any Indians around.

"You all right, Flor?" he asked, concerned.

"You just keep movin'. You won't leave me behind."

They rode most of the afternoon. They had just watered their horses and crossed a little creek when Daniel once more spotted the tracks, moving at right angles to the direction he and Flor had been riding. "Cephus has switched again. Only this time there's a lot more horses. That whole bunch of Indians is trailin' after him."

Flor said, "I can't for the life of me figure why Cephus keeps changin' direction so much."

"Maybe he's tryin' to shake off the Indians."

"Only way he can do that is to flap his wings and fly."

As before, Daniel gave up trying to parallel the

tracks. If Cephus was going to keep changing course, the only way to keep from losing him was to take a chance and follow the tracks, Indians or no Indians. Daniel kept turning his head, anxiously searching the hills around them. Doing this, he nearly missed the tracks when they shifted yet again.

"Daydreamin' ?" Flor chided him gently.

"Daydreamin' hell; I'm tryin' to keep our hair on."

They had ridden in the new direction no more than thirty minutes when the horsetracks skirted around a cedarbrake. Any kind of cover that might hide an ambush brought the hair to a stand at the back of Daniel's neck. He took a long, hard look at the cedar, lifting the rifle up a little from his lap. He saw nothing suspicious, though a hard knot seemed to start at the pit of his stomach. Only when they had ridden past the brush did he finally take a deep breath and ease the rifle back down. He turned to look ahead of him again.

He heard a whispering sound and saw something fly past him. For a second he thought it was a bird, till he saw it strike the ground in front of him.

An arrow!

"Run like hell, Flor," he shouted. "They're after us!"

He didn't have time to tell her twice. He heard a whoop behind them. He drummed his heels into Sam Houston's ribs and made straight for a rock outcrop he could see ahead. It came to him that this could be a ruse, that the Indians behind them might be setting a trap and a dozen others might be waiting behind those rocks. But he saw no other chance.

He heard more whooping and saw another arrow flit past him, wide of the mark. He glanced back once and saw a pair of riders heeling their ponies as hard as they could go.

Daniel and Flor made the rocks and jumped down from their horses, grabbing hard at the reins while they swung around and brought up their rifles. The two Indians saw they had let their quarry get away. They pulled their horses up, shouting in anger.

Daniel's jaw fell. "Them ain't men, they ain't nothin' but kids. We been runnin' from a couple of Indian kids!"

At this distance, he judged the boys to be twelve or fourteen years old, nearly naked, each carrying an undersized bow. Their feet did not reach down to the level of their ponies' bellies. But they shouted insults and shook their bows threateningly like men.

Flor said, "Boys or not, they could do you some hurt."

"Damn kids," Daniel fumed, "I can't shoot one of them."

"They'll shoot *us* if they get the chance."

Daniel stood up, the rifle in his hand, and tried to wave the boys away. "You two, get the hell out of here! We don't want to hurt you!" He knew they wouldn't understand the words, but he thought they should understand his gestures. When they didn't retreat, he shifted the rifle to his left hand, reached down for a biscuit-sized rock and hurled it at the boys. It missed.

In reply they sent two arrows at him. One missed by four or five feet.

Flor remarked, "That boy'll be ready for war paint by next year. You better watch him."

"I ain't taken my eye off of either one." He saw the boys putting their heads together, hastily parleying. Their decision was unmistakable.

"Godalmighty, they're fixin' to charge us."

The two boys put their horses into a run, each reaching back to his quiver and bringing an arrow to the bowstring.

Daniel swallowed. "God knows I hate to do this." He brought the rifle up and sank to one knee for steady aim.

Flor said, "Daniel, you wouldn't . . ."

Daniel squeezed the trigger. The powder flashed in the pan and the rifle roared, smoke belching from the barrel. A horse squealed and went down, its rider pitching headlong out into the grass. The young brave broke his bow.

"Shoot the other horse," Daniel shouted. Flor fired. The second horse fell, perhaps thirty feet past the first one. The boy seemed to have expected it and landed on his feet running, trying to fit another arrow. Daniel stood his ground, knowing he had no time to reload the rifle. When the boy paused to loose the arrow, Daniel dropped. The arrow struck the rock. Daniel tossed his reins to Flor and sprinted out. Using his rifle like a club, Daniel brought it smashing down across the lad's wrists. The bow fell useless.

The second boy was on his feet, rushing with a

knife. Daniel parried the thrust with his rifle barrel and fetched the boy a jarring clout under the chin. The youth staggered a moment, and Daniel jerked the knife from him. He cut the first youth's bowstring and shoved the knife into his belt.

Breathing hard, he turned to confront the two lads. "Damn, but you try a man's patience. What's the matter with you two, anyway?"

Whatever they said was gibberish to him, but he knew he was being roundly cursed. One of the boys rushed at him barehanded. Daniel threw him down and stepped aside. "You boys are fixin' to get me mad." One boy helped the other to his feet. Daniel said sharply, "Look what you've went and done. You've made me shoot your horses, and you're apt to have a long walk home. If you got any enemies out here, them shots is like as not to draw them. I know *we* got enemies. Now the both of you git before I stop makin' allowances for your age. *Git!*" He pointed. They didn't understand the words, but he thought they got the gist of it, the last part anyway. They retreated resentfully, pausing first for another look at him. If looks had been lethal, Daniel would not have survived.

"*Git* now!" he repeated. They retreated a little farther and stopped. Daniel took a hasty look around. He saw no sign of other Indians, but he figured if any had heard the shots, they would certainly be here by and by.

"Let's get out of here," he told Flor. They rode off in

a lope. Daniel looked back once and saw the two boys watching them. "I ought to've wore out their britches."

"They didn't have any britches," Flor reminded him.

There was no question now that they had to abandon the effort to follow the trail of Cephus and Milo. If the shots had been heard, it would likely be the Indians following the silver hunters who heard them. Daniel came to a small creek and reined up in it to cover his tracks, Flor following his example. He looked again to be sure they were out of sight of the two boys, who would no doubt put grown men on their trail if they had the chance.

"Of all the rotten luck," Flor blurted. "We may never find Milo and Cephus now. Two damnfool Indian boys—two rotten kids."

"Anyway, they had guts."

"Their guts may've cost us a silver mine."

They followed the creek for two or three miles, looking for a rocky place where they could get out without leaving tracks. They found a good one, but Daniel decided it was too obvious and passed it up. He rejected three more likely places, finally climbing up and out onto a rocky bench where he thought the hot sun would quickly dry the water they had trailed up with them.

"Hold to the rock as long as we can," he said. "We'll keep them confused."

"Not half as confused as we are."

They paralleled the creek always, watching for a

line of rock they could follow to get away from the creek without leaving sign. Daniel's roan horse started to lift its tail, and Daniel slapped him on the rump to try to make him forget the notion. That would be all a sharp-eyed Indian needed to see. The ploy didn't work. Daniel had to get down, lift a flat rock and rake all the fresh droppings under it, then fit the rock carefully back into place.

He grumbled, "People who brag about how smart their horses are just ain't been caught in a tight like this."

They hadn't gone much farther when he heard hoofs striking against stone, far behind them. His stomach went cold. "They're comin'," he said tightly. "In spite of all we done, they're comin'."

He saw fear grip Flor. For a moment he was afraid she would cry, but she was too strong for that. The only cover he could see was a long live-oak ridge well above the stream. He pointed and started out, picking his way to stay among the rocks as long as he could. He looked back frequently for pursuit.

Flor said weakly, "I wisht I was back in San Antonio, washin' other people's dirty clothes on the riverbank."

"And I wisht I was plowin' my folks' south field. But I reckon we both came into this mess with our eyes open."

They rode into the live oaks and dismounted so they could have the use of their rifles if they needed them. Presently a dozen or so horsemen came working slowly up the creek, watching for sign at its edge.

Daniel muttered under his breath. "There's them two damn boys, runnin' along afoot like a pair of trackin' hounds."

The boys were out a little farther than most of the horsemen, bent over intently studying the ground at their feet as they trotted to keep up.

The horsemen came to the place where Daniel and Flor had climbed out, and Daniel felt his heart begin moving up into his throat. A cold sweat broke out on his face.

The Indians paused a little, and he found himself holding his breath until his lungs were in pain. One of the boys skirted close to the flat rock where Daniel had hidden the horse manure. But the Indians passed on. Daniel let his breath out slowly and wiped his sleeve across his face. He glanced at Flor and judged she was a little sick.

There was nothing to do but hold their ground, for back downstream he could see a couple of straggling Indian riders coming along behind their fellow warriors, perhaps hoping to see something the others had missed. The sun was going down when the Indians came back downstream, making another search over the same ground but a hastier one this time. Again they passed over the place where Daniel and Flor had left the stream. In the dusk, Daniel watched them move away.

He held his voice almost to a whisper. It didn't even sound like his. "They figure we went downstream. Maybe we've lost them."

"Since they're goin' downstream, I'm in favor of goin' *up*stream, just as far as we can get."

"We'll lose Cephus and Milo."

"Right now I don't care if I never see either one of them again, and if I never see a dollar's worth of silver. I just want to breathe."

They rode long into darkness, putting the Indians far behind them. But in so doing; Daniel more or less lost his bearings; he had only a vague idea of direction and a vaguer one yet of distance. They pulled up into timber finally and camped, eating a little dried buffalo meat. Daniel slept but little, and he doubted that Flor slept at all.

At sunrise, Daniel looked upstream and saw something which struck him as strange. Perhaps fifty yards from the creek was a remnant of something built of stone. His first thought was that it might have been an Indian dwelling, but he couldn't remember ever hearing about Indians who built stone houses in this part of the country.

Once he was satisfied there were no Indians around, he rode cautiously toward the structure. He saw that at one time a rock wall had been built up in a circular shape several feet from ground level. Some of the lower side had been washed away, probably by many successive rises on the creek. On the ground above the circular structure lay a huge rock that six men could not have lifted. Grooves had been carved into it. A rotted log lay beside it, badly broken, hardly enough of it left to indicate that once it had been all in one piece.

Nearby lay more stone and the ruins of what had been some type of platform. These rocks were blackened as if they had been burned repeatedly over a long period of time.

He found Flor as puzzled by it as he was. He asked, "You ever seen anything like this?" She hadn't.

Then her eyes brightened in sudden realization. "But I've heard about it. Daniel, I think this is an ore smelter."

He blinked. "What's a smelter?"

"Where they crushed the ore and then melted the good stuff out of it. That circle over there, I'll bet that's the ore crusher. They'd dump the ore in there. That big rock was tied to a log with rawhide, and the log was laid across the top of the wall. Them Spaniards, they'd make Indian slaves push down on one end of the log to raise the rock up, then step back and let it fall on top of the ore. When they had it all busted up, they'd wash it out and then melt down the heavy stuff over yonder where the rocks are burned." Her voice was excited. "You know what this means? We've come onto the place where they melted the silver down."

Daniel's skin prickled. "Then the mine must be around here close. They wouldn't of carried that ore any farther than they had to."

She began to laugh. "That stupid Cephus—while he's off runnin' around over the country like a lost hounddog, we're findin' the mine." Her laugh became louder, and a little wild.

Daniel looked around worriedly. "There might be

Indians back there somewhere behind us."

"And there's a fortune in silver somewhere ahead of us. Come on, Daniel, let's go and find it!"

14

IT OCCURRED TO DANIEL THAT IF THIS HAD INDEED been a smelter and the ore had been brought here from a mine for any great length of time, the foot traffic should have beaten out a trail that probably would not have healed even yet. He discerned what might have been several, but he knew they were as likely to be game trails as any path beaten out by silver miners.

He looked carefully for Indians. Seeing none, he motioned to Flor that he intended to follow one of the trails and see if it led to anything. She nodded eagerly.

This trail led up a slope, through a thin scattering of live oaks, and over the top. He hesitated to go up over the hill and stand the risk of being skylined to the view of searchers far away. Instead, he skirted around and picked up the trail on the other side. It began meandering and breaking down into smaller trails, and before long he realized it was nothing made by man. This was a path the deer and the buffalo had long used working their way down to the water.

Flor was disappointed, but he reminded her there were more trails to try. He picked up another which also played out before long. Daniel and Flor then went all the way back to the smelter and picked up a third that he thought looked possibly heavier-traveled. Before long he realized it was less crooked than the others. Anticipation began building in him again, for he had a feeling about this one. He looked at Flor and saw she had caught the excitement; she had lost her disappointment over the other two. "Don't build your hopes too much," he warned her. But he knew he was wasting his breath.

He heard something ahead and stopped to listen. Brush crackled somewhere up the slope. Quickly he signaled Flor and they pushed their horses down into a clump of close-grown cedar, stepping down to the ground and getting ready to clamp their horses' noses. Dry-mouthed, Daniel watched through the heavy cedar.

At length the tension drained out of him. "Buffalo," he said in relief, "goin' down to water." The animals walked slowly without sign of alarm, which he took as a good omen. He let them plod by before he started to move out of the cedar.

His eye caught something lying on the ground in the cedarbrake. He took it at first for a small, dead animal, then decided it was something else.

Flor said, 'Come on, let's find that mine."

"In a minute. I want to see what this is." He led his horse through the close-bunched timber where the still heat seemed tightly held by the dense foliage; his pushing through it shook accumulated dust from the greenery, and he sneezed.

What he found was a scattering of black metal.

roughly molded into wedge shapes, each bar just a few inches long. He picked one up and found it much heavier than it looked.

Flor pushed up behind him. "What you got?"

"Lead, looks to me like. Lead bars to be melted down and poured into bullets."

Flor hefted one experimentally. "What're they doin' here in the middle of a thicket?"

Daniel picked up a few more of the bars and found beneath them a remnant of badly rotted rawhide. "I'd say they was in a rawhide bag. Rats or somethin' have chewed up the bag except what was underneath." He found a few pieces of ancient wood, which he thought were oak, pieces of a packsaddle. Amid the bars was a flint arrow point, the wooden shaft long since rotted away.

"I'd guess they had this lead on a packmule or a burro. When the Indians hit them, this mule probably got shot with arrows and ran off into the thicket to die. That was a long time ago. Everything has been eaten up or scattered except the lead bars and a little of the packsaddle."

"I bet them Spaniards was wishin' they had this lead cast up into bullets."

"We're liable to all be wishin' the same thing before this trip is over with. I got a notion to load some of this in our saddlebags and carry it with us."

"What we're lookin' for is silver, not lead."

"We may need the lead to let us get the silver and leave here alive."

He found their saddlebags inadequate and rolled some of the bars in their blankets, tying them behind the saddles. "A lot of extra weight," he admitted, "but if we get in a tight, I reckon we can always drop the blankets off and run."

Even so, they left a good number of bars where they had found them, on the ground in the thicket.

The trail led a couple of miles up from the smelter. He almost missed the point where it suddenly turned up a hill. Rains through the years had washed down the rocky hillside, all but wiping out the traces. He pointed. "Up yonder, Flor. I think we'd best tie the horses in the brush and climb up there afoot."

At the crest of the hill he found a large mound of odd-colored earth and rock which did not quite match the ground around it. Part of this had washed down the hillside, leaving a smear of light color which contrasted strangely with the rest of the earth. He picked up a piece of rock three times the size of his fist and found odd scratches on it. Chisel marks.

Flor made the guess first. "This has all been dug out of the earth. The hole it came from has got to be right here someplace." Her voice was high-pitched with excitement. Daniel cast the rock aside.

He missed the hole twice before he found it. A bush had grown up at the edge of it over the years, all but hiding it. When Flor saw Daniel had found it, she rushed over and began hacking at the bush's trunk with a heavy Bowie knife. Daniel thought she was not far short of being hysterical. He took the knife from her and warned her not to get too close; she might fall in. The hole appeared to go almost straight down.

When the bush was cut away and cast aside, he found the hole to be roughly oval in shape, three to four feet across. It was not quite straight down, but the sides were too steep to climb without a rope or some other help. He picked up a small rock and pitched it into the hole to get some idea of its depth, for he could not see bottom. From the sound, he judged it to be twelve or fifteen feet.

"And us without a rope."

"A blanket," Flor suggested, trembling. "We can cut a blanket into strips and tie them together."

Daniel judged Flor's blanket to be the strongest and ripped about half of it apart, testing the strips for strength, then tying them together. He tested the stump of the bush they had cut away and thought it would do for an anchor. Tying one end of the strip to the stump, he dropped the rest down into the hole. "You stay up here," he warned Flor. "If somethin' goes wrong, we don't want to both be caught down there." Cautiously he began a descent. Half-way down he found that footholds had been chipped into the rock wall. That made it easier.

The bottom was farther down than he had thought, possibly twenty feet. He was in what he first took to be total darkness. After he had been there a couple of minutes and his eyes adjusted themselves from the bright sunshine, he could make out the general form of the walls, if it was too dark to see details. He moved cautiously across the room toward a spot where he thought he could see light. There he found another shaft going straight up from the ceiling, barely wider than a man's body. An air-hole, he decided.

He went back to the main shaft and shouted up to Flor. "I got to have light, Flor. Find me somethin' that'll burn."

She dropped down three or four bundles of dried broom-weeds, which she had crushed and tied tightly to make them burn longer. Daniel took out his flint and struck it several times until one of the bundles started to blaze. He held it up and got his first real look at the room in the wildly dancing firelight. It was twenty-five or thirty feet across, just tall enough for a man to stand. He half expected to find a cache of shining silver bars against a wall, but in this he was disappointed. He found nothing but the rubble of hard work. He thought perhaps he would see silver veins sparkling in the walls, but in this also he was disappointed. He saw nothing but rock, the chisel marks still as plain as if they had been made yesterday.

Off in the far side of the room he saw a tunnel, and his heartbeat quickened again. Maybe that was where the silver was stored.

He felt pain and realized that the weeds had burned down to his hand. He dropped them on the floor and went back for a second bundle, setting them ablaze from the remnants of the first one. With the new light he paused in the mouth of the tunnel. He would have to crawl on hands and knees to negotiate it. He looked dubiously at the ancient timber shoring. He feared it was largely rotted away. It wouldn't take much to cause the timbers to fall in, and part of the walls or ceiling might come down with them.

He heard Flor's voice behind him. "Where's the silver?"

He turned and demanded, "I thought I told you to stay up yonder!"

"I couldn't. I just had to come down."

He decided there was no point in scolding her; excitement had such a grip on her that she wouldn't hear a word. "Go bring them other bunches of weeds. We'll need them for light."

With Flor following close on his heels, he went down on hands and knees and began to crawl through the tunnel, careful not to brush against the shoring. Breathing was not easy, for each move raised long-settled dust that threatened to choke him. He saw the end of the tunnel just ahead and reasoned that beyond it was another room, maybe the place where the silver came from. He crawled out of the tunnel and tried to stand but bumped his head against the low, rough ceiling. He took a third bundle of weeds and set them ablaze to throw light across the room.

"Where is it?" Flor demanded. "Where's the silver?"

This room was smaller than the other, no more than ten to fifteen feet across. Here again was an air shaft going up to the top, laboriously chiseled by hand through many feet of rock.

There was no other tunnel; this was the last room. It

was as bare as the first. Daniel reached down and picked up a steel chisel about six inches long, its point pounded to a ruined mass. Halfway across the room lay an old steel hammer, its oak handle broken. Other than that, nothing.

The place was as barren as a robbed tomb.

Flor began to sob, and between sobs she cursed. She took the ruined chisel from Daniel's hand and began to hack at the rock walls until her hands were bruised and bleeding. "Where's the silver?" she cried. "Goddammit, what did they do with it?"

Daniel swallowed a bitter disappointment. "Looks to me like if there was any here in the first place, they got it all."

He studied the walls, thinking perhaps there was a vein of silver here and he didn't know how to recognize it. But he decided he had been right the first time; whatever might have been here, the Spaniards had mined it out before they left. They might have found nothing at all. He fired the last bundle of weeds. "Come on, Flor, we better get out of here while we still got some light."

The weeds burned away before he reached the end of the tunnel, but enough light came from the main shaft so that he could see his way to finish crawling out. Flor came close behind him, crying. On the floor he found a bundle of weeds she had failed to pick up and carry through the tunnel. With his flint he fired these and took a final look around, trying to tell himself he might have missed something. But he knew he hadn't.

Flor bitterly hurled the old chisel against a rock wall. "Fraud," she cried, "that's what it is, a fraud! These damned stupid old men and their damned stupid old stories about buried silver. They're dreamers and frauds, every last one of them!"

The weeds were rapidly burning down, but Daniel was held in morbid fascination by the look of this place. He found one thing half covered with dust: a set of leg irons, badly rusted. He recalled the old stories about Spaniards using the *padres* to Christianize the Indians, and chains to be sure that they did not lose religion. No telling how many had worked and died here. There might not even have been any silver; all that misery might have been for nothing. The place had a smell of decay and death about it. It made him cold.

"Let's get out of here, Flor. This is a bad place."

They climbed back on the dangling blanket strips, Flor going first so that Daniel could catch her if she slipped. Daniel sat outside and rested, letting his lungs fill with the good clean air. Flor sobbed softly again. Daniel decided to hold her and keep silent; maybe the best thing was to let her cry it out and be done with it.

At last he said, "I doubt we can ever find Milo and Cephus again."

He heard something then, in the distance. Gunfire.

Flor looked up suddenly; she had heard it too.

Daniel said, "Looks like *somebody* found them."

"Milo!" she cried. "They'll kill him! They'll kill Milo!"

15

MILO AND CEPHUS AND THE OTHERS WERE IN BAD trouble. Crouching on the crest of a hill, Daniel saw that the San Antonians had taken refuge in a live-oak motte. It appeared to Daniel that they had dug in, shoveling up some kind of hasty breastworks.

They needed them, for in the tall dry grass and scrub oak shinnery around the motte, Daniel counted at least thirty Indians. He thought more likely there were forty, all afoot and well positioned to direct arrows at the men they had surrounded. The Indian horses were being held in safety two hundred yards away.

If the beleaguered Texans had any advantage at all, it was simply that the timber helped deflect the arrows. So far as Daniel could tell, only a couple of Indians seemed to have any kind of firearms. The rifle fire was desultory now. Now and again an Indian would fire a bullet into the trees. Once Daniel heard the scream of a wounded mule. It appeared that Milo and Cephus had lost most of their pack-mules and even some of their horses before they reached the motte.

Flor cried, "What can we do? They're trapped."

Daniel shook his head. "Be damned if I know."

"We got to do somethin'. We can't just sit here and not lift a finger to help."

"I don't know that a whole hand would do them much good. Looks to me like them Indians'll keep them bottled up till they get them all. Far as we know, there may be more Indians on the way."

"From where we're at we could shoot a bunch of them."

"And wind up dead before the others. We ain't even got a stand of timber."

"Well, think of somethin'. We got to save Milo."

"Seems to me like you're suddenly almighty worried about Milo Seldom. Your ol' daddy is down there too."

"My ol' daddy brought this on himself by bein' greedy and mean. Milo Seldom is just dumb; he can't help himself."

Daniel watched, but no idea came to him. For a while it wasn't much of a fight; it was more of a standoff. The Indians were unable to get closer without undue exposure to rifle fire, and the San Antonians were unable to get out of the timber. Now and again someone fired out of the live oak, or an Indian loosed an arrow at what he considered to be a target. It seemed to Daniel that neither side was getting much done.

But in the long run he knew the Indians held all the advantage. Time was their ally, and they had plenty of it.

To one side Daniel saw a wisp of smoke. He took it for gunsmoke from an Indian rifle, but it began to grow. He grabbed a short breath. "Flor, one of them has fired the grass."

The wind was in the Indians' favor. The tiny flame

grew, moving slowly through the grass toward the motte. Indians began shouting their enthusiasm, a number setting fires of their own, blowing on them to get them started, watching them build in the heavy, summer-cured grass. Shortly a dozen fires and a dozen smokes were crackling inexorably toward the timber. The men entrapped there began a faster pattern of rifle fire, trying to keep the Indians down and to halt their grass-kindling efforts.

Tears ran down Flor's cheeks. "They'll burn them out of there. When they try to run for it, the Indians'll cut them to pieces."

Daniel pushed to his feet. "That fire idea ain't bad at all. Maybe we can give the Indians somethin' to worry about. Let's gather up some dry grass and brush."

He had saved the makeshift rope they had made from blanket strips. When he and Flor had quickly gathered a mass of combustible materials, he tied them into two large bundles with rawhide and had enough strip left to drag them by. "Bring up the horses, Flor."

He took out his flint and struck sparks. It required a minute to get the first bundle afire. When he had it burning, he used it to touch off the second. He swung into his saddle and pointed. "You go yonderway. Don't get too close to them." He veered off, putting his own horse into a steady trot down the hillside and onto the long slope that led down toward the motte, the burning grass and brush bouncing along behind him, here and there touching off a blaze. It seemed that the Indians hadn't noticed him yet. He hoped for time. He had to ride slowly enough to let the burning bundle behind him fire the grass; dragged too rapidly, it wouldn't work. He rode straight toward the Indians.

One of them saw him and shouted. Half a dozen arrows were hurriedly sent at him. They would miss, but if he got much closer, they wouldn't. These were no boys. He cut back at a right angle into the thickest of the dry grass, looking over his shoulder. Behind him he was leaving a trail of smoke, the sun-cured mat of ground cover flaming up quickly, the wind rapidly whipping it into a full blaze. He took one glance at Flor and saw she was moving ahead of him on the same general course, moving a little faster and bouncing the burning bundle higher, leaving a more ragged pattern of fire.

Suddenly the Indians on this side of the motte found themselves afoot between two lines of fire—one they had set themselves and the other touched off by Daniel and Flor. Shouting in anger, they sent futile arrows searching after the man and woman. A rifle-carrying Indian shot at them but did not come close.

The Indians were running after them afoot now, some almost as fleet as a horse. Daniel moved into a hard lope, catching up to Flor. "Spur him," he shouted at her. "They ain't overly happy."

Ahead of them was the Indian horse herd. Two Indians guarding it came riding out to meet them, fitting arrows to their bows. Daniel could tell these were young, green warriors, not a great deal older than the two he and Flor had set afoot. Maybe their aim wasn't polished yet.

Flor's bundle of brush and grass burned free of the blanket strips and fell off, but Daniel still had his. He could tell it had the full attention of the Indians' horses, for they stood watching, ears forward, eyes highly nervous as this ominous fireball bounced toward them. The Indian guards' first arrows missed, and Daniel and Flor rushed past. Daniel shouted at the horses, and Flor took up the yelling. Daniel plunged headlong into the horse herd, the flaming bundle close behind him.

That was all it took. The horses broke into a sudden frightened run, tails high, manes streaming. Daniel looked back for the two young Indians and saw only one still on horseback. The other sat on the ground, his horse pitching away in panic.

Daniel felt something hot bite into his shoulder and knew an arrow had struck him. He let the blanket strip go, for the fire was largely burned out. He brought his horse around and painfully reined to a quick stop, bringing his rifle up. He took no time to aim, for he saw the Indian draw the bowstring back.

Daniel fired, and the Indian's horse fell. The arrow went astray.

The horses were in a good run now. It would take awhile for the Indians to round them up. Flor cried, "Daniel, you're hit."

It was beginning to hurt now, the long shaft bobbing up and down with every move he or his roan horse made. He got down from the saddle. He could feel blood flowing warm inside his shirt. Flor jumped to the ground, knife out, and ripped part of the shirt away. "It's not in too deep," she said. "Hold onto somethin'."

She didn't give him much time. He grabbed his saddle, and she yanked at the arrow shaft. It held the first time, and he almost sank to his knees from the pain of it. Before he could do more than cry out, she jerked again and brought it free, breaking the shaft.

He was dizzy for a moment, and realized he was still bleeding. Somewhere in his subconscious he knew some bleeding was good for him because it would wash the wound clean.

He heard a sudden increase in firing but could not focus his eyes to see what was happening. Flor said, "Milo and them, they're breakin' out of the timber. Here they come, runnin' like the devil was after them."

"He is," Daniel gritted, fighting down the sickness that welled up. "I halfway wisht he'd catch them."

"I'll help you on to your horse," Flor offered.

"I'm able to do for myself." But he almost fell over on the other side. He grabbed the saddle and caught himself. Through blurry eyes he saw the men riding toward them, stringing out in a broken line. As his eyes cleared a little, he could tell they had left most of the pack animals behind. They were riding for their lives, and they weren't worrying about baggage.

Angry Indians ran after them afoot, loosing arrows and shouting all manner of insult.

Daniel couldn't see the men clearly enough to recognize them individually, but he knew old Cephus Carmody's voice. "I swear, daughter, when first I seen you ridin' down off that hill, I thought I was killed and gone to heaven. Nary angel ever looked prettier to mortal eyes."

"That's the nearest you'll ever come to seein' an angel, Papa. Everybody make it all right?"

"Bruises and scratches, but nobody killed. Come on, we need to be puttin' distance behind us before we pause to parley."

Cephus jabbed spurs to his mount. Daniel's horse jumped forward to keep up, and Daniel almost lost his seat. He felt strong arms come around him and hold him. A familiar voice said, "Hang on tight, friend Daniel."

Daniel gritted, "Goddamn you, Milo, let me fall and I'll stomp the liver and lights plumb out of you."

He gave all his attention to staying in the saddle. Eyes blurred, he sensed rather than saw the broken land flying by beneath his horse's long-reaching legs. At length he was aware that Cephus and the others ahead of him were slowing down. He heard splashing, and he felt Milo Seldom stopping his horse. "All right, friend Daniel, ease down here into this creek. The wetness of it'll do you good."

The cool water did help. They ripped the shirt some more, and he felt gentle hands washing the wound. He heard Flor say, "It's about quit bleedin'. He won't die on us." Then her voice changed from confidence to sudden concern. "Milo, your face! You're wounded too."

Daniel's vision cleared some. He could see Milo shaking his head, and he could see it streaked with blood and swollen and blue. "Indians didn't do this. I was havin' me a fight with your ol' lyin' daddy when them Indians come up and hit us unawares."

"A fight? What about?" she demanded.

Milo said bitterly, "Tell her, Cephus."

The old man began to back away. "Now, daughter, you don't want to be listenin' to the likes of Milo Seldom. The truth was never in him."

Milo said sharply, "What would you know about truth, you ol' whisky-soak? You never told it in your life."

Flor had taken charge again. "All right now, you two, I want to know what happened. Somebody tell me before I take and shoot you both!"

Milo said angrily, "We wasn't two hours from the San Saba ruins till I knowed the old reprobate was lost. All of yesterday and this mornin' he took us ever whichaway, cuttin' back and forth like a rattlesnake track. He kept sayin' he knowed what he was doin', but he didn't. Finally me and Lalo Talavera shook the truth out of him. That's when me and Cephus had our fight. I tell you, I smote him hip and thigh."

"The truth?" Flor pressed. "What're you talkin' about?"

Lalo Talavera said in Spanish, "The truth, my pretty little flower, is that your father never was with James Bowie on that expedition. He wanted to go, but they would not let him; they knew him too well. He trailed them, but somewhere near the ruins he lost them, and he never did find them again. When Bowie and his men were having their big fight with the Indians, your fine, sweet father was wandering around out here by himself, lost."

Flor took two angry steps toward her father. "Papa . . ."

Defensively Cephus backed off some more. "Now, daughter, I always knowed I'd been within a hundred yards of that mine. I could feel it in my bones. I always figured if ever I could come back, I'd find it; you know I've always had a sixth sense about such things. I could find it yet if I just had a little time, and people wouldn't be bayin' on my heels like a bunch of mean hounds. You got to have a little faith, daughter."

"You know as much about faith as you know about truth, Papa." Daniel thought for a moment that Flor was going to strike her father, but instead she gave him a cursing the likes of which Daniel had never heard in his life, using every possible invective from two languages. When at last she was wrung out, her arms went limp at her sides. She paused for breath.

"Papa," she said, calmer now, "do you know what you've done? You've kept us fired up for years on false hopes about a mine that don't even exist. You've led us out here and put all of us in danger of bein' killed for a wild dream. Your rich mine is a lie. Me and

Daniel, we found it. It's as empty as a promise from Cephus Carmody."

Old Cephus' mouth dropped open. "You found it?"

"We found it. There's nothin' there, Papa, nothin' but just a hole in the ground."

Milo Seldom slumped. "There's *got* to be somethin' there, Flor."

"Lies, that's all we found there. Wild stories dreamed up by people too lazy to work and dreamin' of findin' somethin' they could have free for the takin'. It's just a dead empty hole in the ground."

Daniel could see the impact hit them all, the bitter disappointment of a dream shattered at their feet like glass. Lalo Talavera turned and walked away slump-shouldered, muttering about all the *señoritas* that could have been his. Notchy O'Dowd stood in building anger, fists knotting as his face reddened. Of a sudden he bawled aloud and lunged at Cephus Carmody, and the two men went down together in a rolling, punching, gouging heap. Milo Seldom pushed forward to stop it, but Flor caught his arm. "Leave them alone. One's about as dirty a fighter as the other one is, and they both deserve whatever they get." Her voice softened. "You all right, Milo? You sure you didn't get hurt none?"

"Sure, Flor, you know nothin' ever happens to ol' Milo Seldom. I'm too smart to let it." She touched his leather sleeve and found a fresh hole there, and a thin edge of red.

"Oh, that," he said sheepishly, "just a little scratch is

229

all. One of them Indians had a rifle, and he sort of nicked me a little when I was gettin' Armando Borrego out from under his shot horse. Nothin' serious."

Voice soft and concerned, Flor said, "Take that shirt off and let me look at it. You never know how bad somethin' like this can turn out."

Daniel watched them, listened to the care and softness in Flor's voice, and knew that the arrow wound was not the only one he had suffered here.

One of the Borrego brothers had ridden out on a short scout. He soon came back to the stream in a trot. "Some of the Indians have recovered horses. They are trailing after us."

Daniel thought he had regained enough strength to hold himself in the saddle. Now that he could see clearly, he discovered that several men were riding double, their horses lost. Only one packmule had been salvaged.

The Indians had come out of this thing with a considerable net gain, he thought with an odd detachment; they had a dozen or so packmules and evidently several horses as well. The hell with it all!

The fugitives rode into the night. So long as daylight lasted, they could always look behind them and see fifteen or twenty Indians trailing just out of rifle range. Old Cephus complained, "Ain't they had enough yet?"

Milo told him dryly, "They're lookin' for a grayhaired scalp of one lyin' old windbag to hang up on a shield so the wind'll blow the bullets away."

The horses were tired, and so were the men. Shortly after dark, they made dry camp in a protective rock outcrop which gave them a view of sorts across an open flat and might keep the Indians from slipping up on them in the night. Daniel's shoulder was fevered, but in spite of it, he managed some fitful sleep. The last thing he clearly remembered was hearing Milo tell Flor they had lost most of their ammunition on the packmules. Through the night a vague worry about ammunition kept coming back to Daniel. At other times, in a fevered haze, he would see Lizbeth Wills, and that farm they had planned to own.

The pain of the shoulder brought him awake before full daylight. He looked out across the flat and saw no Indians, but a feeling in his bones told him they were there. He got up stiffly and scooped out a small hole, gathered up some dry grass and small pieces of wood and built a fire in it. He got his bullet mold from his saddlebag, and a wedge-shaped bar of the black metal he had found near the old Spanish mine. He ringed the little fire with stones so he could balance the ladle across it. He put the bar into the ladle to melt the lead down.

Flor came up and sat quietly beside him. "You all right?"

"Fair to middlin'. How's Milo?"

"You know him; you couldn't kill him with a club."

"Yesterday," he said, "I was sore tempted to try, the way you carried on over him. I thought you said you didn't have no feelin' left for him."

231

"I thought I didn't. But then when I saw there was danger of him bein' killed—" She looked away. "I'm sorry if I led you astray, and gave you notions about me and you. I really thought I was shed of him, but I reckon the feelin' has been there too long to get rid of it. God help me, it looks like I'm stuck for life."

Daniel said, "You know how he is; he's got a restless foot. He don't have nothin', won't ever have nothin', won't leave nothin' permanent when he's gone."

"He leaves tracks. He goes where other people ain't ever been, and they see it can be done. They follow him, and *they* make somethin' permanent. I reckon he serves the Lord in his own way."

Daniel shrugged, and the shoulder hurt him. "Maybe so. I think this trip kind of got the roamin' out of *my* system."

"If we get out of this—if them Indians don't get us all—what'll you do, Daniel?"

"Go back to the farm, I reckon. Work for my daddy, or work for somebody else, and hope someday I'll manage to save enough money to take up a place of my own."

"That sweetheart back there—is she a good farm girl?"

"Lizbeth?" He hadn't thought much about Lizbeth lately. Last night was the first time in weeks she had intruded even in his dreams. "Farmin's the only life she's ever known. She's always said she'd be patient and wait. It's always been *me* that was impatient to have a place of my own. But I don't know if I could ever go back to Lizbeth now, not after me and you . . ."

"You'll forget me once you're with her again. We're not made right to live together, Daniel. You're a man who'll have to have your own way, and I'm a woman who's got to have hers. You need a woman who'll follow you but not push you. Milo needs a woman who'll follow him but yank him up short when he goes the wrong way; he needs a woman who'll mother him when he needs it and give him hell when he needs *that*. And I need a man who'll let me do that and get away with it. You wouldn't, Daniel, not very long."

Daniel guessed she was right, but he couldn't be that objective about it yet, not till he'd had some time. He didn't want to talk about it. He looked impatiently at the bar in the ladle. "I don't know what's the matter with that lead. Ought to be meltin' by now. Maybe the fire's not hot enough."

He put a little more wood under it. He saw Milo stirring, crawling sleepily out of his blankets. "Marry him and he'll drag you all over hell and half of Georgia."

"Only when I want to go. I'll give him enough rein to roam where he has to, but keep it short enough that he'll always come back to me. I'll never turn him flat aloose like my mother did with ol' Cephus."

Still the bar showed no sign that it was going to melt. Daniel took out his hunting knife and poked at the part resting down in the hot ladle. "Not even soft," he said disgustedly. "Them Spaniards sure did use a sorry grade of lead."

Flor's eyes widened. "Let's see that bar."

Daniel lifted the ladle off the fire and set it down on the bare ground. Flor dumped the bar out into the dirt, took Daniel's knife and began to scratch at it. He saw that her hands trembled. She looked up, her eyes excited. "Daniel Provost, me and you are blind!"

"What do you mean?"

"We were lookin' for big silver bars, nice and shiny. But if you put a piece of silver up for a long time, you know hat happens to it?"

"It turns black."

"It just came to me; I've heard San Antonio merchants talk about the silver bars the Indians used to bring to trade with. They didn't look like silver till they was polished up. They was rough cast, and they had sat so long they had turned black on the outside." She kept scratching at the bar until some of the inside was exposed. "Daniel, this ain't no lead bar. This is silver!"

"*Silver?*"

"Sh-h-h, not so loud! No use lettin' everybody hear about it."

"But if this is silver, I reckon they got a right to a share."

"Why? They cut us off, remember? They didn't find this stuff, *you* did. By rights it's yours, ever bit of it."

Daniel swallowed. He had no idea how much these silver bars might be worth. He hadn't even counted to see how many he had brought along. Of a sudden he remembered the many he had left behind where he had found them, and he felt sick.

234

"Flor, I couldn't find that place again, not in a hundred years."

"You won't need to. Maybe you got enough to get you that farm. Let the land give you its own treasure, one crop at a time."

His head swam with the intoxication of the idea.

"Half of it is yours, Flor. Don't argue with me; I wouldn't have it no other way." She seemed inclined to protest but didn't. He said, "You can have them silk dresses after all."

She thought about it awhile, then shook her head. "No, I've done without them this long; I reckon I'll live without them the rest of my span. But Milo ain't ever to know, Daniel. You know how he is; there'll come times we'll really be in need and I can go dig up a bar. He won't ever know but what he provided for me himself. He's not too smart, Daniel, but he's a man with pride."

Milo Seldom knew how to make a healing poultice to put on Daniel's wound. He shaved bark from young live oak trees, boiled it down to a syrupy mix, pounded up some charcoal from last night's fire and put it into the syrup along with a little cornmeal for thickening, then slapped it on the wound, binding it up with buffalo hide. "Now, friend Daniel," he promised, "when we take that off in four-five days, you'll be as good as ever was."

They knew San Antonio lay southeastward, so they struck a straight course in that direction. For the first four days they were never out of sight of Indians, who trailed behind them like wolves after a handful of crippled buffalo. Every so often some young warrior, perhaps trying to prove his bravery and bring up his status in the eyes of the tribe, would charge forward alone and send an arrow flying after the fugitive silver hunters.

The first time, Notchy O'Dowd brought his rifle up. So sternly that he surprised himself, Daniel commanded, "Don't shoot him. No use killin' one without need; they'd swarm over us like bees."

O'Dowd obeyed him without question, which also surprised Daniel. He had not intended to take charge, but he found that he had; he found the others waiting expectantly for him to give the orders. It occurred to him that no one else in the party had any better right, or was better qualified. He found himself sitting straighter in the saddle.

Late on the fourth day the Indians fell away. Daniel learned the reason shortly before dark when he saw a group of horsemen approaching on the trail ahead. He ordered his party to dismount in a small stand of timber and prepare to fight if necessary. But presently Milo Seldom said, "Friend Daniel, them ain't Indians; they're white men."

The bedraggled party remounted and rode forward. They found Paley Northcutt there with twenty men from San Antonio; a mixed group of Americans, Mexicans, a Frenchman and a black freedman.

Paley Northcutt was the first to speak. "Milo," he asked eagerly, "whichaway's the silver mine?"

Sheepishly Milo said, "Boys, we never found no silver mine. Oh, there was a mine, all right, but there wasn't no silver in it."

The San Antonians were disappointed. It developed that Paley Northcutt had gone back into town after Flor had sent him away. He had proceeded to get drunk and tell about the planned expedition to the Bowie mine. In no time he had collected a set of eager volunteers, ready to share in the glory and the wealth.

Daniel said, "It's a good thing you came, Paley, even if there ain't no mine. I don't know if them Indians intended to let us get back to San Antonio alive."

It didn't take long for Milo Seldom to tell the whole story, upon which some of the newcomers were of a notion to hang Cephus Carmody to a nearby live oak. But Cephus talked them out of it.

"Boys," he said, "I know there wasn't no silver in the mine that my daughter and Mister Provost found, but that don't mean there ain't another one. Stands to reason them Spaniards didn't dig one hole and quit. Stands to reason they had more than one mine— maybe a *dozen* of them. Somewhere out yonder is a mine with a pile of silver bars taller than a man's head, bigger'n a Mexican *baile* room, maybe bigger'n *two* of them, just waitin' for the taker. I swear, boys, soon's I can get me an outfit together and some good men to ride with me, I'm goin' back out there and find that mine. I'll go right to it the next time; I got a feelin' now that I know just where it's at."

He got them out of the notion of hanging him.

Before he was through talking, half of them were of a mind to turn around and go back with him.

Milo had his arm around Flor's shoulder. "You know somethin', Flor? Ol' Cephus makes sense. I bet you, the next time we can . . ."

Flor looked hopelessly at Daniel and shrugged. "Milo . . ."

"What, *querida*?"

"For God's sake, Milo, take me home!"